FOOTPRINTS
IN THE
FROSTING

FOOTPRINTS
IN THE
FROSTING

Laura Pauling

Redpoint Press

For information visit www.laurapauling.com

paperback ISBN-13: 978-1511658102

paperback ISBN 10: 151165810X

Summary: Holly Hart starts her new life in Fairview to discover a
body in the kitchen of her cheesecake shop, and she's drawn into the
murder investigation to save her company and her reputation.

Edited by Cindy Davis

for all mystery lovers

SOMETHING WAS WRONG.

Early morning light trickled through Holly's cozy apartment, and she desperately tried to hold onto the fragments of a good dream. Her scalp prickled, a tingling that spread down her neck. She startled awake.

With narrowed eyes, she studied her small room, filled with flea market finds. The antique dresser barely fit, but Holly fell in love at first sight with the blue paint, chipped enough to reveal the white underneath. So what if there wasn't enough space in the tiny room for anything else? When she first saw this apartment, directly across from her new business, *Just Cheesecake*—she couldn't turn it down.

Her gaze flitted about the room as she tried to figure out what felt wrong. The tiny doggy bed next to hers was empty. Muffins!

No wet nose nudged her awake this morning. She let out a huff of frustration. That dog! Ever since she'd left home to strike out on her own, that cute, tiny, mangled ball of fur had transformed from obedient-watchdog-with-a-sixth-sense-for-danger to runaway-train-wreck at every opportunity.

Quickly, Holly wrapped her pink and black polka-dotted robe around her latest purchase of cotton pajamas, the top and bottoms covered with tiny frogs. In the store, when she'd looked closely, the googly eyes and pink tongues won her over. Plus, she'd wanted to invest in the local economy of her new hometown.

"Muffins!" She called for him several times while searching her apartment, which didn't take long. He wasn't under the bed or in the bathroom or waiting by the door to be let out. "Muffins!" She hoped he'd magically appear. "Bad dog," she muttered.

In the kitchen/living room, she stopped short. The door to her apartment hung open a crack. Her keys hung on a hook in the wall. She'd stumbled in late the night before and never locked up. She must not have even shut the door all the way! Early morning air seeped through.

She raced to the large window by her table-for-two—another flea market find. He wasn't anywhere to be found. Holly searched across the street and saw a flash of gray.

"Muffins!"

It was still early, probably not even six a.m. She could dash across the street, catch her little runaway, and be back before anyone noticed. Her grand opening was at nine.

Her grand opening!

She smacked her forehead. How could she forget? That had been part of her dream, tons of customers and cheesecake flying from the shop as if it had wings.

Without hesitating, she slipped into her flip-flops—a little chilly for this early in May—and ran onto her small deck, down the wooden steps to the dirt driveway. She shared the tiny parking space with other tenants. Not many cars were on the road this time of day, so she sprinted across the street.

After several minutes peeking behind and under the few cars parked in the small lot, Holly stood with her hands on her hips. He was nowhere. Out of breath and feeling frazzled, she plopped down on a stone bench. That dog! Several evil thoughts passed through her mind about what she should do to him, but she immediately dismissed them. Muffins was her one link to her parents. Regardless of his recent bad behavior, she had a soft spot for him.

Letting the cool morning air calm her down, she couldn't stop the giddy feeling or the smile at the sight of her shop. The large red and yellow banner above the entrance screamed Grand Opening. She'd worked hard for several weeks, preparing for today. Her shop was nestled between a charming restaurant, *Oodles*, and a touristy gift store, *Gotcha*. Perfect. She'd hopefully get lots of foot traffic. Especially since she'd signed a contract with the restaurant to provide the cheesecake they offered on their menu.

Her thoughts wandered to the competing bakery a little ways down the street. She bit her lip. Hopefully, the owners were reasonable, and they wouldn't hold a grudge. A little competition was healthy for everyone.

Or it would put her out of business before her business venture had a chance.

4

"Hello, there. Are you lost?"

She stiffened, remembering she was still in pajamas. Heat from a blush spread rapidly across her cheeks. She looked up to find what most women would consider to be an incredibly good-looking man. Chestnut hair fell in soft waves around a classic handsome face. His ruddy complexion gave him the appearance of youth, but she figured him to be at least a few years older than her twenty-two years. In her previous life—the one she'd escaped—she'd had enough of suave, handsome men to know they couldn't all be trusted. And this guy fit the bill. From the manicured nails to the pressed suit and tie.

"I happen to know exactly where I am." She stood, hoping to gain a little dignity, but he still towered over her by a foot.

He smiled, cautious but friendly. "That's good to know. I was just making sure." He stuck out his hand while studying her attire. "The name's Mason."

She forced a laugh and shook his hand. "I'm Holly, and I don't normally parade around in my PJs, but my dog escaped."

"Maybe he craved a cup of coffee. Shall we go see?"

She laughed. "Sure." Mustering every ounce of dignity required to strut about in PJs, she walked with him across the parking lot and into *Oodles*. Her mother would absolutely fall over in a faint if she could see Holly, undignified and dressed in nightclothes.

Inside, the smell of dark brews and breakfast greeted her. Would Muffins have ducked through when someone opened the door? "See a tiny gray dog with mischief stamped all over him?"

Mason looked about as if he owned the place. "Nope. But let's get some coffee. We'll keep an eye out."

They walked to the counter. As they passed the community bulletin board, Holly noticed again, the invitation to a murder mystery book club. As soon as she had time, she'd grab the phone number.

"We're getting stared at," Mason said. "Do I have toothpaste on my tie? Did I forget to tame my bed head?"

She laughed. "Oh no, it's me. Look at me."

He stepped back and sized her up. "I don't know what you're talking about." He smiled. "I thought frogs were trending in women's clothing."

"Right. Let's order and get out of here."

Holly ordered a medium coffee with a vanilla swirl and sugar. Mason asked for a mocha and a Danish.

He pointed to a small table. "Shall we?"

Hmm. This was turning into more of what seemed like a date. She slid into a seat. "Everyone's looking at me. Maybe I should leave?"

He sipped from his to-go cup. "Nah, you're with me. No one will say a thing."

"A little cocky, aren't we?" She knew his type, and even though so far he'd been nice, it was only a matter of time before his true colors showed.

He lowered his head in humility. "Some might think so but I hope you'll get to know me before judging me by the clothes I wear or the size of my house."

His words softened her heart. She knew what that was like too. People assumed she was snooty because of where she used to live. No one would think that of her now, not in this little town and not with her tiny apartment and her cutesy pajamas. She smiled. "How do you know I already don't know you?"

"This town's pretty small. I know a new face when I see one. Have you met many people so far?"

She sighed. "Not really. I've been so busy settling into my apartment and preparing for the grand opening, I haven't really had a chance."

"Oh. So *Just Cheesecake* is yours?"

"Yup. You'll stop in later, right?" At least she'd have one customer.

"Definitely. I'm in town early for business. But I'm glad I came or I wouldn't have bumped into you."

Holly hid her blush behind her cup and quickly changed the subject. "Why don't you tell me about some of the people to watch out for then."

He nodded toward a man with a long Santa Claus beard. "That guy over there is the worst. Definitely trouble."

"Why?" she whispered, leaning over.

He glanced right and left and leaned so their faces were inches apart. "I'm kidding. He's my family's lawyer, and he's the jolly old man he looks like. In fact, he might really be Santa Claus. He's probably waiting for me."

She sat back, acting disgruntled, but she couldn't fake it for long. "Anyone else?"

He offered a weak smile. "I'm probably not the right person to ask. Most seem to shy away from me."

Holly nodded, flashing back to her years of living in her parents' influential neighborhood. There always seemed to be a wall between her and everyone else. Developing friendships took longer than usual.

The door opened with a whoosh. An older lady clomped inside. Her graying brown hair looked like it hadn't been combed. Her yellow rubbers reached to her knees like a storm was about to blow through any minute. "Who's that?"

"That's Charlene, the crazy cat lady."

Holly watched with interest as Charlene tacked a piece of paper to the board and then clomped back out. "She seems like a no-nonsense kind of person." Holly already liked her. She could use honesty in her life. No more lies and deceit.

"You could say that." He tapped his watch. "Not sure how much longer Santa's going to wait." He stood. "Nice meeting you, Holly."

"You too."

***

OUTSIDE, ALMOST FORGETTING about her PJs, Holly saw a flash of gray dash into her shop. Muffins? Her shop should be closed and locked. That was odd.

9

Ignoring the curious looks, she walked across the more crowded parking lot and peered into the window. The insides lay in darkness. In a few short hours, hopefully, the place would be busting with business. At least Mason promised to stop by, her one and only friend so far in the town of Fairview.

After a moment of hesitation, shocked at the broken lock on the door, she pushed it open and stepped inside. She tried to ignore the growing sense of dread. The place seemed empty. Quiet. Normally, the black and white tiled floor and retro tables and the counter with the glass showcase below brought her peace and satisfaction.

Muffins whimpered from the kitchen.

The same sense that wakened her from sleep this morning, returned. She crept across the floor and stopped in the doorway to the kitchen. Paw prints trailed across the tiles. She reached over and pressed her fingers against it. The creamy texture felt familiar. She sniffed it. Frosting. Her buttercream frosting she made for her special deluxe cheesecake. Triple the sweetness.

How had Muffins gotten it on his feet?

She flicked on the light. His prints in the frosting led to the back corner, where he sat whimpering. Next to him laid a body, facedown in one of her deluxe cheesecakes.

THE ROOM BLURRED. A body in her kitchen? Frosting all over the floor. A squeamish feeling churned in her gut. Immediate compassion for this man flooded her. Who was he? Was he a sugar-addict who broke in for his latest fix and tripped? She stifled a giggle. That would make for a rather humorous headline. But then she looked at the odd way his body was splayed across the floor, and the way his limbs lay still, and how he would never be able to breathe with cheesecake in his nostrils.

Was it…could it possibly be…murder?

She stumbled back out of the kitchen, trying to erase the image of the body, unmoving and lifeless, and her cheesecake all over the floor. She needed to find help. At the front door she stopped. "Muffins!" That dog.

Feeling guilty—and she didn't even know why—she crept back to her kitchen. "Muffins!" she hissed. "Come here."

Muffins scratched his nose and whimpered. He placed a paw on the body. Almost as if he was protecting it. A little too late for that.

Holly tried a different tactic. "Come on, Muffins. Time for breakfast." She crouched. "You can have one of my cheesecake muffins." She continued to tease him with the foods he loved. Treats she normally refused to give him. "Be a good boy and you can have a treat every day for the rest of the week."

Muffins stared back at her, his eyes questioning, almost as if pleading with her to take action. What in the world did he expect her to do? Solve the murder and apprehend the murderer within the span of minutes while he guarded the body?

Enough. Swallowing the guilt lodged in her throat for possibly disturbing the crime scene, she tiptoed across the kitchen floor. That thought hit her hard. A dead body. In her kitchen. Ignoring that disturbing thought for the moment, Holly stepped over the body, cringing, then she picked up Muffins. "Oh, you bad dog. What am I going to do with you?"

Holly had moved to this quiet town wanting peace and quiet and the busy life of owning and operating a small business. This was the last thing she expected. With Muffins nestled in her arms, his warm body comforting her, she nuzzled her face against him. He whimpered again.

"I know," Holly whispered. "We have to tell someone. But who?"

Since she'd first dashed across the street, the parking lot had filled considerably. Her legs wobbly, she stumbled back into *Oodles* and stood in the doorway, confused. Images of the body flashed through her mind. She swayed while searching the shop. Mason sat in a corner booth with his family lawyer. Everyone else, she didn't know.

Someone bumped into her. Holly barely acknowledged it, a bit too shocked at the murder scene in her kitchen.

"What's wrong with you?" a crackly, raspy voice spoke next to her. "You're as white as the sheets on my bed."

"A body," Holly whispered.

14

"What's that you said? I'm sloppy?"

Holly snapped out of the shock to look at the woman next to her. It was the same woman with the yellow rubbers who'd stomped in here earlier. There was a sparkle of life in her eyes and a rosy flush to her cheeks. Her appearance was plain and simple, but something Holly admired. She'd had enough of snooty dressing to last a lifetime.

"You're a fine one to comment on my sloppy way of dressing. Who cares if I like to dress for comfort?" She clutched the sleeve of her flannel shirt. "This here is the softest flannel around. Humph."

"What are you talking about?" Holly asked, bothered that she'd offended this lady. "Aren't you Charlene?" Mason had called her the crazy cat lady.

"Oh great. Just terrific." Charlene rolled her eyes. "I don't even get a chance to introduce myself and someone's already shared the juicy gossip."

"Well, I wouldn't—"

"What'd they say?" Charlene stuck her face close enough that Holly could see the fine laugh lines around the woman's eyes. "That I'm crazy? That I run around town talking to myself in the middle of the night? That I collect cats like people collect coffee mugs? Well, that just figures you'd believe them before giving me a chance. But don't worry. Old Charlene is used to it." She smoothed her flyaway hair, her eyes studying Holly. "Just remember that I'm not the one wearing my pajamas around town. Be careful or rumors will spread about you too."

At that moment, Holly could care less about her pajamas. Okay, well, maybe a little. "First of all, I said body not sloppy, and second, I only heard about the cats." Holly wisely chose to leave out anything about crazy.

Charlene didn't stop. "If you'd lost your husband, and then your only son moved out, you'd want some company. You might take in stray cats to chat with late at night. You might be called crazy too." She narrowed in on Muffins and rubbed his head. "Cute little thing. Needs a bath though."

"Never mind." Holly sighed.

Charlene seemed to hear only what she wanted to hear. Maybe Mason would help. She hated to interrupt what was probably a business meeting.

"Wait a second." Charlene's arm flew out and dragged Holly back. Her gaze darted between the customers in the cafe. "Did you say something about a body?"

Holly nodded.

16

Charlene dragged her to the closest table and practically forced her into the chair, then she sat in the opposite one and leaned in, her gaze intense and curious. "Tell me everything. Why'd you do it? Was it a crime of passion? A lover cheating on you?"

"What? No!" Holly hugged Muffins closer.

"How about revenge, then? How long have you been planning it? You can trust me." When Holly didn't answer, Charlene rambled on. "Or maybe your past followed you here. You ran away to a small town to hide out and someone found you."

Holly gulped at how close Charlene came to the truth about her running away.

"This isn't your first brush with death, is it?" Charlene leaned back and glanced out the large window into the parking lot. "I can tell these things. I see it in your eyes."

"You do not!"

"Yup." Charlene tapped her head. "Old Charlene knows these types of things. Too bad you dragged an innocent animal in on this."

"Muffins had nothing to do with it."

"Ha!" Charlene pointed a knobby finger. "So you admit it?"

"No!" Holly almost shouted.

Charlene shook her head. "Tsk. Tsk. Getting flustered. Red face. Escalating anger. All signs of guilt."

Holly stood, the anger burning bright now. "I've done nothing of the sort. I came over after finding a body in my kitchen to ask for a phone to call the police. I left mine back in my apartment when Muffins went missing this morning. All you've done is misunderstand me and throw around false accusations like you're some sort of detective. Maybe you should turn up your hearing aid."

"Found a body, you say?" Charlene stared, triumph on her face, and for the first time, she didn't ramble.

Holly's back prickled as the door to the cafe closed behind her. A glance at the tables revealed that her outburst had drawn an audience. Mason and his lawyer stared. A couple of old ladies fanned their faces with their hands, murmuring. The barista stood at the espresso machine, the hot liquid spilling over on the floor.

"Or did you murder your past lover and plan to *discover* the body and stumble in here all innocent?"

"Okay, that's enough." A deep voice spoke behind her.

Holly whirled around to find a cop, his keen eyes piercing her, suspicion floating around him like a cloud. He

18

was only a few inches taller than her, but the air of authority he carried with the uniform and the gun strapped onto his belt made him feel five feet taller than her. She visibly jerked at the sight of him, dislike growing inside her. Not every cop was trustworthy. She backed up.

"Where do you think you're going?" Charlene asked when Holly bumped into her. "Trying to escape? I thought you might. That's when I called Trent."

"I said, that's enough," the cop practically growled. "You said something about finding a body?"

The murmurs and whispers escalated. All of a sudden *Oodles* felt about a hundred degrees warmer. Charlene had called the cop? The pieces fit together. The old woman had rambled on, forced her to sit, and wasted time with her made-up theories all to keep Holly here while the cop zipped over, probably from his morning donut fest. Holly had fallen for it like a six-year-old sitting on Santa's lap at the mall.

"Yes, I did."

Some of the customers gathered around, curious and whispering.

Trent, the cop, leaned close. "Why don't you show me this body?"

Holly gulped, glancing at her clothing. Frosting lined the edge of her right flip-flop. She must've stepped right into the evidence when she picked up Muffins. That dog! Silently, she took back the part about offering him extra treats.

"Amateurs." Charlene huffed. "Always making stupid mistakes. Leaving evidence behind...or wearing it."

Holly brought Muffins closer to her chest. This didn't look good for her. At all.

LIKE A PARADE, everyone filed out of *Oodles* and across the parking lot to Holly's shop. At the sight of the grand opening banner stretched across the door, her insides crumbled. An ominous feeling—and the fact that a dead body laid in her kitchen—told her that the grand opening would be postponed.

Charlene bopped along beside her. "What? Is the act of passion finally catching up to you? Feeling regret?"

Holly restrained herself from shoving the old lady, whether she owned cats or not. She kept her mouth shut. She'd already made herself look bad once.

At the door to the shop, Trent turned around with typical cocky cop swagger. Holly bit back the rising panic. This was really happening. "Okay, folks. This is as far as it goes. The morning excitement is all over. Go back to your normal business."

"Hey!" someone cried out.

Along with everyone else, Holly turned. A bright flash nearly blinded her. She blinked and tried to find the guilty party, but all she saw were the curious faces of the townspeople who now thought she was guilty of murder.

"Or," Trent muttered, "you can read about it in the town paper tomorrow morning."

Holly cringed. She would look the crazy part. Mangy dog clutched in her arms. Messy hair.

Trent pushed opened the door to her shop. The scent of cinnamon offered little comfort to Holly. She didn't want to see the body again.

She pointed to the kitchen door, her hand shaking. "He's back there."

As Trent moved forward, Holly stayed glued to the spot. There was no way they could think she was guilty. So what if she had frosting on her flip-flops? She had to rescue her dog. Anyone could see that.

Charlene stuck to her side. "I'll make sure she doesn't try to escape."

Trent sighed as if Charlene nosed around in a lot of the cop's affairs. As Trent investigated the crime scene, Holly stood with Charlene in awkward silence.

"Murder isn't so good for opening day, is it?" Charlene asked.

"No." Holly stared at her glass cases, filled with cheesecakes and muffins and cupcakes. All for nothing.

"Definitely a crime of passion. No one would be stupid enough to plan a murder that would sabotage her opening day of business. I wanted one of the muffins, too."

"Or maybe I had nothing to do with it, and I'm telling the truth? Did you ever think of that, crazy cat lady?"

Charlene burst out laughing. "I knew you were lying. You've heard all the rumors. I'll be keeping an eye on you."

Trent walked out, his face grim. "Let's take a trip downtown, shall we...what's your name?"

"Holly," she said in a quiet voice. "Holly Hart."

Trent placed a hand on her arm. "Well, Holly Hart. Welcome to Fairview."

***

EVEN THOUGH THE police station was only a mile away, to Holly it felt like a long trip. Lonely too. The sights of the town passed before her eyes. A deep longing welled inside. This was what she wanted. Life in a small town. A few good friends. Practically being accused of murder definitely put a slight crimp in those plans.

She tried not to catch the cop's eyes in the rearview mirror. They both suffered through the awkward silence until he pulled into the station. "Let's say we go inside."

"Will I need a lawyer?" Holly asked.

His eyebrow rose. "Only if you think you need one. I just have a few questions. After all, the body was found in your shop. Ignore Charlene. She loves a good mystery." He opened the door and stepped outside. Holly followed suit. Close to the front door of the station, he said, "If you'll wait a minute. I have phone calls to make first." He gestured to a few chairs in a small waiting room.

"Sure." At first she sat in the chair, perched on the edge, back straight. The stale smell of coffee and the stereotypical box of donuts brought her back to reality. Her shop would not have its grand opening today. In fact, she might never have a customer. Even Mason, when he found out about the murder, might not show up. She allowed the self-pity to swirl around until she remembered that someone had been murdered. At least she was still breathing.

Desperate for comfort, Holly was willing to try even police station coffee. She grabbed a cup, placed it under the Keurig, and punched the button. Soon, she sat back in her chair and tried to relax. If she didn't murder the man, who did? And who was the victim? If she needed to clear her name, she at least needed the basic facts. For the first time, she breathed easily about meeting with the cop. She had just as many questions for him.

The door opened, and a warm spring breeze wafted through. Charlene waltzed in, a smug smirk on her face. Holly tensed and sipped the weak coffee.

Charlene plopped down in the chair next to her. "Nerve-racking, isn't it?"

Holly stiffened, biting back a retort.

"It might be easier to confess to me, your only friend in town, than with a cop. They just make you nervous and trick you into confessing."

"That's on television shows." Friend? When exactly did this lady think they became friends? She'd engaged her in conversation until the cop showed up. Probably worked for him.

"Oh, really? We'll see about that."

"Really." Holly sat quietly. The doubts at Charlene's statement flooded through her.

The cop opened the door to his office. He frowned at the sight of Charlene. "What are you doing here?"

Charlene stood, not backing down. "I figured Ms. Holly Hart would need a friend. Someone on her side, so she doesn't end up in the clinker."

He sighed. "We don't throw people in the clinker when they're innocent."

"Someone needs to be in her corner." Charlene crossed her arms.

The door opened again. A petite blonde with a short pixie cut breezed through. She wore skinny jeans, a blue button-up with a matching scarf. Her black boots reached her knees.

The cop let out a huff. "Not you, too. I'll be making a statement later."

A statement? Holly noticed the audio recorder in the girl's hand, and the camera swinging from her shoulder. She must've taken her picture earlier. Maybe she could beg for a retraction if this girl really was a reporter.

With an airy walk, the woman sat on Holly's other side. She smiled, the warmth reaching her eyes. She stuck out her hand. "Hi, I'm Millicent."

"Hi." Holly shook her hand, the first person this morning, since the whole incident, to offer a smile.

"What a horrible welcome to the town, you've had. I've been meaning to stop by and say hello."

"I bet you have," Charlene muttered and grabbed a magazine from the small table next to the chairs.

Millicent ignored Charlene and kept on talking. "I hope you've managed to find everything. We're not a huge town, but everything you could need is on Main Street. And there are the hidden spots in town, the hiking trails, the viewpoints. Places that only the locals know about. Have you found those?"

"No, not yet." Holly tried to hide her frog pajamas by closing her robe. "I've been busy working."

"Oh? Where do you work?" Millicent beamed with curiosity and interest.

Holly ignored Charlene's snotty huff. "*Just Cheesecake.* I was supposed to open today."

Millicent squealed. "I noticed that shop. What a cute idea!"

The cop cleared his throat, silencing Millicent. "Holly, if you would come on in."

Charlene stood as if to enter, but the cop stood firm and shook his head. Holly walked into the tiny office a bit more relaxed after chatting with Millicent. She seemed the friendly sort of person, and someone who would know the people of the town. She'd be a great place to start with questions to clear her tarnished name.

Before the cop shut the door, he said, "Both of you can go home."

Inside, Holly sat across from the desk. The cop took his seat in front of it. "First of all, let me apologize for this morning. I hate for introductions to happen like this. I'm Trent Trinket."

"Hi." For the first time Holly took a closer look at Trent. He was surprisingly young and fairly good-looking. Not in the suave, polished manner like Mason who exuded wealth

28

and privilege, but in a small town mama's boy kind of way. The kind of son who stacked wood for his parents and still stopped by for Sunday dinners. A family kind of guy. Honestly? Holly was tired of the good-looking wealthy guys, even having them as friends. Trent's sandy blond hair was cut short, and he had a youthful face, dimples and everything.

He pulled out a pad. "What can you tell me about this morning?"

This question shocked Holly back into reality. Despite his youthful appearance, he was still a cop, and probably knew how to use his innocent look to his benefit. With a deep breath, she dove into her explanation: Muffins had escaped, and she'd seen him across the road, so she thought she'd dash over and grab him. How she met Mason and got sidetracked.

"Wait," Trent said. "Back up a second. Did you mention Mason Carlton?"

"I don't know his last name."

"Hmm. Interesting."

"Why?" Holly perked up. Trent knew something.

"Oh, nothing. Continue."

She explained about finding Muffins in her kitchen and how she had to enter to rescue him, thus the frosting on her flip-flop. When she finished, she let out a breath and leaned back in the chair.

"About that. We'll have to take the flip-flop as evidence."

"But, but..."

He smiled. "Sorry about that."

"If you're going to make me waltz about town in my bare feet, at least tell me who was murdered." Even if she wore PJs, she wanted to maintain some sense of dignity.

He pressed his lips together and studied her before speaking. "His name was Ralph Newton. He works on staff for the Carltons."

"Oh." She wondered if Mason knew yet and how he was handling it.

"You do realize, Ms. Hart, that you shouldn't leave town." He paused, then said, "And I'm sorry, but we'll be in your shop for at least the rest of the day and most likely tomorrow."

She deflated. "Okay. Can I go now?" If she had to postpone her grand opening, she could use that time to her benefit. "If the murder is solved soon, will I be able to open?"

"Well, yes, but—"

Holly was already standing up and out the door only to come to face to face with Millicent who barely masked her surprise at being caught eavesdropping.

Holly smiled, but Millicent was like a bloodhound, and without a second look, pushed past her into the office. "I have a few questions, Officer Trinket."

The door closed.

Holly rubbed Muffins between the ears. "What do you think? Should we stay and listen?"

He looked toward the door and wagged his tail.

"That's what I thought."

AT FIRST, FEELING a little guilty, Holly stood casually outside the office. If someone walked inside, they might question why she chose that spot, but they wouldn't assume she was spying. After a few minutes of this and afraid she'd lose hearing valuable information, she inched closer to the door. The voices were muffled, but she caught a few words. One word in particular. The Carltons.

She strained, guessing that Millicent knew something. Maybe Trent would let something slip. If only, they'd left the door open a crack. That would've made her life easier.

"Might as well put your ear to the door. Works a lot better," Charlene whispered. "Then you can tell me what they say."

Holly startled and whipped around. "I thought you'd left."

"Nope. Just taking a pee break. My bladder isn't what it used to be, but I have no intention of wearing those old people diapers. I'm not that far along yet."

"Um, okay. Thanks for sharing." Holly wanted to laugh at Charlene's honesty. It was a fresh breeze even if she over-shared.

"Go on." Charlene motioned. "See if you can hear anything worth our while."

Holly narrowed her eyes. Was this another trick? "You're trying to get me in trouble, aren't you?"

"Better you than me."

Muffins whimpered, almost as if to nudge her back to the task at hand. "I know. You're right, Muffins. No distractions."

Charlene huffed. "And you call me the crazy cat lady."

In a loud burst, Millicent's voice rose above their mumbling. After a tiny shove from Charlene, Holly inched closer to the door and laid her ear against the wood, listening.

"There has to be something to this. It can't be coincidence," Millicent stated.

"If I let you share your theory, will you leave?" Trent sounded worn down, ready to give up. Holly wanted to giggle.

"Yes," Millicent said. "Promise."

Trent's voice dropped lower than Holly could hear. She felt a poke in her side.

"What's going on? Anything good? They reveal the killer yet? If it isn't you, that is," Charlene said.

"Hold on. I'm listening." Holly pressed a little harder against the door while clutching Muffins to her chest. He'd better not bark or scratch at the wood.

Millicent was talking. "I've been around a while, longer than you in this town. I know things. I see patterns. Good reporters always do. And whenever the Carltons show up on the scene or try to play their hand, something goes wrong."

"Unlike reporting, detective work is based on fact, not assumption. I can't tail the Carltons or investigate without reasonable doubt or because a reporter tells me she knows who committed murder."

"What about Ralph? Longtime community member. Kind. You don't think that one of the staff dying, smothered by cake, is cause for reasonable doubt? Sometimes servants overhear information not meant for them. Sometimes they get greedy. Sometimes they blackmail."

Charlene tugged on Holly's sleeve. Holly held up a finger. Trent and Millicent were getting to the good part.

"Well, I wouldn't say that," Trent stuttered before continuing. "It's definitely something we'll look—"

A hand on her arm, Holly felt herself being yanked away from the door. Charlene whispered, "Tell me what's going on."

"They're still talking!"

"Tell me."

"I don't know," Holly said. "They weren't finished. Something about the Carltons and business and murder."

Charlene crossed her arms. "Well, duh. We knew that beforehand. Now get back to listening before they finish."

With a slight huff of exasperation at Charlene's statement after she'd pulled Holly away from listening, she pressed her ear to the door again.

"That's preposterous! Walter Huffly is one of the most respected men in town." For the first time, Trent's voice was loud and clear. "This is what I mean by fact. Waltzing in here and throwing around accusations like its candy at a parade. I've had enough."

"Time to skedaddle," Charlene whispered. "Trust me. There's a time limit to these things. Best to get going with the little information we have."

"Hold on." Holly ignored the warning to leave. Just a few seconds more. Who was Walter Huffly? Did he have something to do with the Carltons?

Millicent spoke even louder. "What about Holly Hart?"

Holly gasped, then clasped a hand over her mouth. Muffins nipped at her arm as if encouraging her to leave.

"The first suspect should always be the one most closely connected to the murder. In this case, the scene of the crime. Who is Holly? Where did she come from? Maybe she has enemies here or some longtime vendetta. Did you think of that?"

"Please leave the detective work to the police."

"Just because you see a pretty face and a single girl in town, doesn't mean you can neglect your duty." Millicent's voice grew louder.

Holly panicked, realizing Charlene had been right. Before she could leave, the door opened, and she fell forward into the office.

"Case in point," Millicent said. "Why else would she be hanging out by the door spying?"

Trent and Millicent gave her the stare-down. Holly fought the heat rising in her cheeks, and not for the first time, wished she'd never left the house in her pajamas. Never again! "I-I was talking with—" She turned to reveal Charlene, but Charlene had vanished. Left when she'd urged Holly to do the same.

"Don't worry," Trent said drily. "I assume someone else put you up to this."

Even though Charlene hadn't been all that kind, Holly felt a loyalty to her. Maybe because she loved cats. Maybe because so far, she'd been the one Holly had talked to the most. Maybe because she didn't care what others thought of her and stated her mind without regret.

"Sorry." Holly offered a humble smile. "It was just me. And I was listening because I heard my name. Given the present scenario, is that too hard to understand?"

"No, not at all, Miss Hart. But if you don't mind, this was a private conversation."

"Like I said." Millicent smiled smugly. "Another pretty, eligible female can cause distraction. But don't worry, I'll make sure the investigation hunts down the killer. Now if you don't mind I was in the middle of an interview." Millicent nudged Holly out of the office and shut the door.

Holly stumbled back. She needed a breath of fresh air to cool off. Minutes ago, this nice, pretty reporter had befriended her. Smiled. Chatted. Welcomed her to the town. What happened?

"Psst!"

Holly snapped out of her reverie. Charlene stood at the front door and crooked her finger, motioning for Holly to come outside.

Without a glance back, she left the station. The air had grown warmer, almost warm enough for cropped pants. The sun shone. It would have been a wonderful grand opening. Now? A corpse lay in her kitchen. She was a murder suspect by default, and she'd made it worse by spying.

"Told you it was time to skedaddle."

Holly said the first thing that came to mind. "You know, rain boots aren't really necessary. The sun is out." She pointedly looked at Charlene's feet.

"Ha!" Charlene pointed a finger at her. "You're one to talk. Wearing pajamas meant for two-year-olds and strutting around town in them."

"But look." Holly shoved her arm sleeve close to Charlene's face. "Look at those googly eyes. And the cute way the frog's tongue is flicking out. How could I not?"

Charlene laughed. "Look at us. Arguing like two old biddies." She cracked her back. "I've been standing too long. Might as well sit." She hobbled to a stone bench.

Holly noted that Charlene could move fast when she wanted and just as easily played up the old lady stereotype when needed. But, she did have a point, and it was unkind of her to make a crack about her boots. Holly sat next to her. "I'm sorry. You're right. That was unkind."

"He's kind of cute, isn't he?" Charlene asked, her eyes sparkling with mischief.

"Who?"

"Officer Trinket, of course. He's one of the town's hotties."

Hotties? Holly giggled. "He's okay." Holly remembered the way Millicent seemed to grasp for any theory, however wild, and throw it out there. Or maybe that had been her plan. Put it all out there and see which one caused a bigger reaction in Officer Trinket.

"We can talk about your love life another time. What we need to cover is your deplorable skill in detective work." Charlene rubbed at her knees, then waited for a response.

Holly sighed. "Go ahead. Tell me everything I did wrong. I know you're dying to."

"I wouldn't joke around about dying today," Charlene scolded, but there was a hint of a smile.

"I don't even want to think about it." Holly buried her face in Muffin's fur. "Thank God I have you, little buddy."

Charlene cleared her throat. "Number one rule when eavesdropping. Get in and get out. There's always the temptation to stay longer to glean more information. Be happy with a nugget, then skedaddle. Stay any longer, and one way or another, you'll get caught. Which you learned today."

Holly saluted in jest. "Thank you for the lesson."

"You're welcome. Any time. You might have potential." Charlene glanced at her watch. "Talk about the time. Time for me to mosey on out of here."

Before Holly could say goodbye, Charlene had practically sprinted to the sidewalk with a bounce in her walk. Guess the old-lady hobble wasn't needed anymore. Holly smiled. She couldn't tell if Charlene would turn out to be a friend or enemy. She seemed to appear and disappear with perfect timing.

The front door of the police station opened, and Millicent breezed out, cool and collected, even after her heated conversation with Trent.

Talk about perfect timing.

HOLLY HAD MINUTES to compose herself. Her feelings toward the suave, chic peer wavered between gratitude, hurt at being betrayed, and awe that Millicent, in the span of minutes, could create such a reaction in her. Desperately, Holly thought back on the conversation she overhead. Something about a Walter, about the Carltons, about business, about Ralph. Holly barely remembered which name to attach to the victim.

All too soon, Millicent stood next to her, silent but present.

Holly scrambled for something to say, anything. Muffins growled and nipped at the air.

"Ooo, what a cute doggie!" Millicent reached out to pet Muffins, but the dog yipped at her.

"Muffins. Bad boy." Holly pulled his head away and moved him to the other side of her. "Sorry about that. He's usually nice to everyone."

"No problem. I'm not much of a dog person." She sat and fake-wiped sweat from her brow. "Phew. That was a bit cray cray in there, wasn't it?"

Holly studied Millicent. She smiled. She seemed sincere, acting like all the horrible things she said to Trent about Holly hadn't been said.

"Those are the cutest jammies."

Holly still didn't say anything, still hurt, still confused, her tongue tied.

Millicent slumped over. "Fine. I'm sorry."

"Sorry for what you said about me or sorry you got caught?" Holly asked, her voice hard and sharp. She even surprised herself.

"Sorry that you overheard. I know you're innocent and so doesn't Trent. That's my approach with him. Overwhelm him with so many theories and questions that he lets something slip. Keep him off balance around me so he loses composure. It's worked before."

"That's okay. I didn't hear much. Voices were too muffled." Holly plastered on a smile, attempting to cover her white lies. "Mainly I heard you accuse me." This was also a good time to fish around about this Walter guy. "And something about Walter?"

Millicent waved, like she was shooing away a fly. "Oh, him. Just my attempt to make everyone look suspect. Like Trent said, Walter is one of the nicest men in town. Plays Santa Claus every year at the Christmas parade. Donates generously to local charities. I'd be more suspicious about his employer, the Carltons."

The information clicked with Holly. The man with the beard, Mason's family lawyer. He must be Walter. And he was tied in with the family business. "Why Mason?"

Millicent tilted her head, questioning. "I didn't say anything about Mason. Have you met him?"

"Um, yes, I did. This morning."

"Why? Was he acting suspicious? In a rush?"

"Oh no. Not that I could tell." Holly giggled at their spontaneous meeting. "Unfortunately I was still in my pajamas when I met him. You don't like him?"

"He's nice enough, I suppose," Millicent said. "I'm suspicious of anyone with money. Where there's money, there's motive. That's my motto."

"I'm off the hook, then." Holly laughed. "Because I don't have any money."

Millicent laughed too. "Neither do I. So, are you enjoying Fairview so far?"

Holly thought back on the last few weeks. It had been hard getting everything in place for *Just Cheesecake*. Hard but exhilarating. She'd been so busy with work she'd barely had a chance to meet anyone other than realtors and town selectman. And now cops and reporters. "Definitely. I've been busy, but I'm looking forward to getting into a routine so I can explore the town."

"Oh, right. You're the owner of that cute little cheesecake shop. You're brave."

"Why?" Holly didn't associate bravery with specialty desserts.

"Well,"—Millicent shrugged—"the businesses in that space have come and gone. One will open for a few years and then close, unable to make a profit. Focusing on cheesecake would make it even harder. Especially with a fantastic bakery down the street."

Cheesecake always got Holly excited. "I noticed that cute bakery. I guess I didn't see my shop as competition. Cheesecake is in its own category. It—"

"You know the bakery sells cheesecake, right?"

"I hadn't thought about that. Anyway, competition is healthy for the market and the economy."

"Yes, but that bakery has history. The owner's family has lived in town for generations. Small towns have loyalty."

Holly squirmed. Millicent made a good point. Maybe before settling in Fairview Holly should have done more research. She hadn't had the time, and she'd fallen in love with the scenic town. Too late now.

"I'm sure you'll last for at least a couple years. If you're lucky."

Holly deflated. What a morning this had been.

"Gosh, I'm so sorry. Here I am crushing your dreams when you haven't even had your grand opening. That was today, right?"

Holly shook her head. "Yes."

"It must have been quite the shock this morning when you found the body."

Something snapped inside Holly. All the worries, the trauma, the rush of the emotional day caught up to her. Her throat thickened, her eyes teared. "Yes. It was awful. I've put in so much work. Everything was ready to go. And then this happened. It's the worst thing that could happen on opening day for a business."

"I wouldn't say that..." Millicent said.

"Okay, tell me one thing that would be worse?"

"Um,"—Millicent fiddled with her purse—"A fire? A bomb?"

"A zombie apocalypse," Holly said, laughing.

"A vampire attack." Millicent laughed, too.

"A blizzard."

"Alien spaceship landing and crushing your shop."

They both continued laughing, tears of frustration turning into tears of laughter. Slowly it dwindled. Holly felt encouraged.

In the quiet pause in their conversation, she had a new thought. It had been the first thought she'd had this morning on finding the body.

"Spit it out," Millicent ordered. "You've been struck with a thought. I can tell these things. Years of investigative reporting."

"I'd dismissed this thought earlier, after I found the body. But why my place? Why my shop? A crime always has motive. Who would want my business to fail?"

Millicent squeaked. "Could it be sabotage?" She lowered her voice. "That the competing bakery wanted to make sure you failed?"

Holly gazed off toward the center of town, where the crime scene unit was investigating right at that moment. "I don't know. Maybe. It's a possibility."

HOLLY SAT, SLUMPED over at her tiny table-for-two. So far, her day had been a disaster. When she'd dashed out of the house that morning, she thought she'd be back in minutes. Then her morning exploded.

Starting with murder. Or what could very possibly turn out to be murder.

Muffins whined at her feet, nudging her into action.

"You must be starving." Holly moved to get the dog food from under the sink and poured it into his dish. "Here you go. So sorry about that." She crouched next to him as he

49

attacked the food. "Guess we both had a tough morning. You went outside for a second, and then our whole morning disappeared. Poof!"

As she watched Muffins eat his breakfast, she wondered about the fact that she'd found him, in her kitchen, with the body. And why would someone commit murder—or plant a body—in the kitchen of her new shop? "You know everything, don't you?"

Muffins looked up from his water dish and barked.

"Too bad I can't understand dog talk. You're probably the only witness, and I know more than everyone how smart you are." She could only imagine talking to Officer Trinket and asking him to allow Muffins to sniff through a line-up of guilty suspects. He already thought she was a suspect. "But I have bigger problems."

She left Muffins to go shower and get ready for the day. While washing off the sweat and trouble from her morning, her thoughts wandered back to the murder. She'd read enough mysteries to know that every crime had to start with the victim. What was he like? Who had problems with him? And after that, move onto those in his closest circle. Usually, murder wasn't random. Find the reason. Find the killer.

Millicent's words returned to her. "Where there's money, there's motive." And the Carltons had money. From what she could tell a lot of it. Maybe she'd need to arrange a coincidental meet-up with Mason again. Offer her condolences.

Standing in front of her closet, she tapped her chin. The next time she met anyone she'd be dressed properly. Cute. Fashionable. Time to make up for running around in her frog pajamas—as cute and trendy as they were. Maybe tomorrow, everyone would start wearing them. She giggled at the thought of Charlene dressed in pajamas, except hers would have cats on them. She thought about Officer Trinket. What kind of pajamas would he wear? Hmm. She'd have to think about that.

Eventually, she slipped into white-cropped jeans with a sunflower yellow top, short sleeves and a sloping neckline. Until further notice, her flip-flops were evidence, so she slipped into sandals. Before she visited Mason, she had to visit her shop. Hopefully, she'd find good news. That the investigation was done, and she could get back to baking.

After adding a spot of blush and some lip-gloss, Holly headed to the kitchen, which only took about five steps. Muffins stood at the door, panting.

51

She laughed. "Couldn't you have done your business while you were out causing trouble this morning?"

He whined as if to apologize.

"Oh, don't worry about it. Maybe if I take you for a short walk, the chances of my shop being free and clear will be higher." Holly grabbed his leash, clicked it onto his collar, then proceeded out of her apartment to Main Street. The sun had climbed much higher in the sky, the heat warming up the air since early this morning. "I knew it would be a beautiful day." Quite ironic considering everything that happened.

They walked down the street. Holly thought back to the victim and the grief his family must be going through. She could relate to that. "No one deserves to lose a loved one prematurely," she whispered. "No one."

Muffins tugged on his leash, pulling her along.

"How far of a walk do you need after this morning?" she scolded gently. "You should be exhausted and ready to sleep the rest of the day."

He tugged again.

She looked between her shop and Muffins. He'd caused enough trouble today. "No," she said firmly. "Do your business, and we'll head home. I have to salvage something from this day."

When her dog actually listened and obeyed, heading back toward their apartment, she felt bad for being hard on him. Like her, he was adjusting to a new home, new town and surroundings. Maybe she'd buy him some doggie treats later.

At the door, she leaned over to unclip the leash. As soon as she did, Muffins took off running down the street.

"What?" Holly stood aghast. Her nice, small dog had turned into a terror. She sprinted after him. "Muffins! Come back here." Forget the doggie treats.

Instead of running back to *Just Cheesecake* or the other stores, he headed in the other direction. For a small dog, he was fast. Holly chased him up and down a maze of side streets, constantly calling for him and threatening him with exaggerated punishments.

He didn't stop.

When he cut through the woods, Holly wanted to cry. She was wearing sandals! She forged ahead anyway. What kind of wild animals were in the woods of a small town? Overgrown brush scratched at her exposed legs. Dead trees, hollowed out by rot blocked some of the path. She dodged and ducked, all while trying not to lose him.

Thirty minutes later, and what felt like a gazillion miles from town, Muffins dashed down a private driveway. Stone sculptures decorated the entrance. Terrific, she thought. Just what these owners wanted—a mad dog and his flustered owner prancing through their private property.

At the end of the long driveway, a mansion towered above her. It had to be at least three floors. Everything was pruned and painted to perfection. A four-car garage stood off to the side. For a tiny moment, she felt the pang of missing home and all she left behind. No, she told herself firmly. She knew all too well that many secrets lie behind fancy houses and numerous vehicles.

Muffins turned a corner and headed to the back of the house. Holly stopped to catch her breath. The owners might not notice a dog, but they'd notice her trespassing across their gorgeous lawn. Maybe she could sneak around the edge of the yard to the back.

Or maybe, after one crazy dash, she should creep along the landscaping close to the house. Just what she wanted to do today, crawl through mulch in white pants!

That seemed her best option, other than ringing the doorbell with her convoluted story. They'd probably call the police. Not what she needed—another run-in with Officer Trinket even if he was kinda cute. She shook off that thought. Where had that come from?

Desperate to find Muffins and leave, Holly sprinted across the grass. Halfway, a sandal fell off. Not wanting to risk being seen, she made a dash for the cover of the landscaping, a smattering of bushes and flowers.

In front of the window, she noticed movement and ducked. Was that Mason she'd seen? Crouched below the window, sweaty and tired, her white pants soaking in the moisture and dirt from the mulch, she contemplated her situation. If she were at the Carlton residence, was this a coincidence? Had Muffins led her here to find a clue? What if they had murdered a staff member? What if Mason's act of kindness and friendship this morning was a cover? Or what if he felt guilty about ruining her opening day?

The crunch of tires on gravel snapped her from her thoughts. When Officer Trinket stepped from his cruiser, she cringed and crawled over to a large bush. Just what she needed.

He regarded the house in true cop fashion, taking in details, observing with a keen eye. He narrowed in on something and then crossed into the yard.

Her sandal!

He picked it up and scratched his head. She tried to shrink in on herself, become invisible. Then Muffins trotted around the corner, straight to her.

"Go back!" she mouthed, knowing it was futile. He hadn't listened to her all morning.

Officer Trinket chuckled. "Well, what do we have here? I assume your owner is here somewhere. You might as well step out Holly."

HOLLY FELT ANNOYED for several reasons. One, she'd gotten caught spying for the second time that day by the same person. Two, she'd wanted to peek in the window and see what Mason was doing. Maybe she'd almost stumbled upon case-breaking information.

Officer Trinket spoke again. "I have your sandal. I see you crouched in the bushes. And I have your little dog, too." He laughed at his own joke.

Hilarious, Holly thought.

"I can't help but wonder why you're here. The last time I saw you, you were spying in your pajamas. Though, I see you've decided to dress like a normal person. The time before that you were practically admitting to murder."

Holly couldn't keep back her comment if she'd wanted to. His words pricked and poked at her, pushing her to her limits. She stepped out.

With fire in her words, she said, "And who are you to jokingly accuse me of murder without looking at any hard evidence?" She narrowed her gaze in on him, her background with dirty cops spurring her on. "Who knows, Officer Trinket? Perhaps you are the one caught in a muddle. Maybe you're related to the ghastly crime, accepting bribes to be quiet, and now you want your money? Arriving by day, in hopes that no one would notice your casual saunter to visit the family who employed the victim. I smell a rat."

His eyes bulged. He sputtered out nonsense. He gaped. He tried to remain composure.

"You look rather guilty to me," she said, her tone light and airy but laced with accusation.

"That is quite enough, Miss Hart," he stated, his face reddening.

"Oh, so now we're back to formalities. I see how you like to play the field. No more joking and flirting now that I see through your charade. I don't care if you are one of the most eligible bachelors in town. I'm not shopping."

"Flirting?" His mouth flapped open, letting out nothing but gasps.

Holly knew she should stop. She knew her accusations were a result of her experiences and this morning's humiliation. She knew he could be here to talk with the Carltons because they employed the victim.

A new voice entered the mix. "I hate to interrupt a lover's quarrel, but may I ask what either of you want?" Mason stood in the doorway. "Last I checked, this was my private property. Last I checked, there was a no trespassing sign at the end of the driveway."

A champagne glass dangled from his fingers. Holly also noticed when he turned and handed it to someone inside. Champagne means celebrating.

"Well, Mason, don't you think it's obvious?" she asked.

Both men looked at her. Officer Trinket still attempted to regain his composure and dignity, and Mason studied her with amusement.

"There was a dead body found in my shop this morning. A man,"—the name came back to her—"more precisely, Ralph Newton was his name. Officer Trinket, when not unfairly harassing citizens, is probably here to ask you some questions since Ralph was employed by your family. So hopefully, you have an alibi."

"And what about you?" Mason asked, leaning against the doorway, a twinkle in his eyes.

"I'm here because my dog ran away. He's the most important witness in all this, since he, most likely, observed the murder. Funny, that he led me here. I wonder why..."

Mason lost his grin.

The door opened, and Walter Huffly appeared, taking in the scene. "What's the commotion?"

A man stood in the shadows behind him.

Holly wanted to step closer to get a better look, but she'd outstayed her welcome. Her anger had fizzled, and she desperately wanted to escape. She grabbed at Muffins who dodged her grasp.

Mason laughed.

"Muffins! Come here." For the one and only time that day, her dog bounded toward her. She picked him up, and without another word, whirled around and marched down the driveway for her long trek back to town.

***

THE NEXT MORNING, after a miserable night's sleep, Holly sat on the couch, in her pajamas, staring vacantly at the wall, in full zombie mode.

The news she'd received the evening before that she couldn't open *Just Cheesecake* until further notice, the fact that she'd accused two men of wrongdoing with no proof, the fact that this whole experience dredged up her past with murder—all of this had her completely depressed.

After an hour, Holly shot up from the couch. Stewing in self-pity was not in her character. She strode to her bedroom, got dressed, taking care to add a bright scarf to her outfit— anything to put on a good show. She needed—no craved—a latte from *Oodles* across the street. Maybe a change of scenery would pull her from this slump.

"And no, you're not coming with me," she said to Muffins who cowered by his breakfast bowl.

61

Entering *Oodles*, she breathed in the aroma of coffee and breakfast. Definitely a good decision. She could already feel the peace and joy rekindling. She was living her dreams, and she could never forget that.

"Hello, there. We seem to be bumping into each other everywhere." The twinkle was back in Mason's eyes. And did he ever look good. His casual business attire fit perfectly and brought out the color in his eyes. The daily newspaper was tucked under his arm.

Holly stiffened, her accusations from the day before screaming through her head.

He smiled. "All will be forgiven if you have breakfast with me. I hate eating alone."

She didn't have an answer. Why would he want to have anything to do with her after she implicated him in murder?

He rambled on about the day and community activities as if nothing had happened yesterday. He followed her up to the counter where she ordered a skinny vanilla latte and a croissant, then he followed her to the corner table.

"Do you mind?" he asked.

"Go ahead." She slid into the seat. Maybe she should've stayed in her apartment.

She let him talk, noticing the quiet stares of the customers, and the hushed conversations. She sipped her latte, the yummy goodness warming her insides.

"Is everyone staring at us, or is it me?" she interrupted him.

Without even glancing about, he said, "Oh, definitely they're staring at us. We're the talk of the town. Though, I'm no stranger to that." He opened the paper.

Neither was she, though she'd hoped to escape all that with her new start. "Sorry about yesterday. I let my words get away from me. And I was embarrassed and upset."

He studied her over the paper. "And I'd been hoping that a pretty girl like you was stopping by for a visit after I'd charmed her with my wit and good looks."

"You're kidding, right? I about accused you of murder. Remember? I trespassed on your property. I caused a scene."

He waved her off. "Forgotten."

She was dumbfounded. How could he write all that off? He should be furious.

"Of course I'd be questioned by the police. We expected it." Pain crossed his face. "I feel for Ralph and his family. He hadn't worked for us very long, but he was a good worker.

Trusted. Loyal." He paused, smiling. "And you were adorable chasing after your dog."

She couldn't help but laugh. "I wouldn't go so far as to say that."

"I would. And to prove I hold no ill feelings, you must agree to go out with me sometime. Not even an official date if you don't want to call it that. Let me show you around town since you're new."

She stared at her half-eaten croissant. A friend would be nice. A boyfriend? She wasn't sure she was ready for that.

"Everyone needs a friend," he stated, while reading over the paper. "And it looks like you could use one." He pushed the folded newspaper across the table so she could read it.

The headline on the first page was in all capitals, big and bold to make sure no one missed it.

Just Cheesecake? Or Just Murder?

Local shop owner guilty of frosting more than cake.

HOLLY COULDN'T DO anything but stare at the bold headlines that falsely accused her of murder. Murder! A large picture of her accompanied the article. She looked terrible. Hair a mess. Pale face. And her frog pajamas. Her eyes skimmed the paragraph, while she gripped the table, anger flooding her.

Small town charm appeals to many people, but along with the idyllic setting of coffee shops, bakeries, and bookstores hides malice, jealousy, and the desire to get ahead.

Earlier this week, a body was found in the new shop, Just Cheesecake. Everyone was surprised that someone would be willing to invest in another bakery, especially after the longstanding historic success of The Tasty Bite. Now we are aghast that this new shop has brought crime into our lovely town.

Ralph Newton, the victim, was a hard working family man with a wife and kids to support. For him, it was wrong place, wrong time. Possibly stopping in town for a cup of joe on his way to work.

In a moment of duress during an interview, newcomer and shop owner, Holly Hart, suggested foul play on the part of The Tasty Bite. That somehow, the shop, fearing competition, had something to do with this tragedy.

Holly crumpled the paper in her hand. "This is an outrage!"

"That bad, huh?" Mason offered an encouraging smile.

"Worse than bad. Millicent planted thoughts in my head then twisted my words." She glanced back at the title. Local shop owner guilty of frosting more than cake?

A flicker of knowledge passed across Mason's face before he quickly masked it. "Who wrote it?"

"Millicent Monroe." One of Holly's first female friends in town. She'd been so nice yesterday, cheering her up, chatting with her. Then she turned around and did this. Her compassion outside the police station had been nothing more than a play for information, for an admission of guilt. "It's my fault. Thinking that small town life would be different. That everyone would be trusting, open, and friendly.

"You must be a city girl?" Mason asked.

Holly thought about the life she left behind with a twinge of sadness. "I wouldn't exactly call it city life. Just a different life." Not that she could explain her past to anyone. That had to stay secret. She didn't want to finish the article but knew she must. She smoothed out the wrinkles and continued reading.

Let's hope the Fairview Police work fast and efficiently to catch the killer. The truth always surfaces eventually. And as for Just Cheesecake? We'll just say that the Grand Opening day didn't turn out so grand.

Mason tugged the newspaper from Holly's grasp. "So you don't tear it up. It gets worse?"

Holly slumped over. "Not really. More of the same." Why did Millicent have it out for her? She must've been serious when she mentioned Holly's name to Officer Trinket the day before. Then, looking for a scoop, she'd faked the start of a friendship. "I shouldn't be surprised. That's what reporters do."

Mason touched her hand. "Sure. But they're also supposed to report the facts, not add in their own unproven theories." He skimmed the article then looked at Holly. "Did you really suggest that *The Tasty Bite* committed the crime?"

"No. Yes. I mean no." The day had finally caught up to her, and Holly had lost it. Of course she cared about the victim more than the fact her opening day had been ruined. But couldn't she be upset about both? "I broke down in front of Millicent."

Mason laughed. "You showed weakness to a reporter? Mistake number one. Never reveal your emotions."

Holly ripped off a chunk of the croissant. "I know that, but she was nice. I was upset."

"Yes, but showing emotion, revealing that chink in your armor, only leads to attack. I've learned that in business the hard way." Mason folded the paper and waved it. "But don't forget, this is to get a reaction, to shock the public."

Holly finished her croissant while Mason read the paper. The silence was comfortable, but Holly was in turmoil. The murmurs, the whispers, floated around her.

"Are you the owner of the small gray dog?"

The question startled Holly from her thoughts. Walter Huffly stood before their table with a smile, his protruding belly bumping her latte.

"Muffins?" Her stomach sank. She didn't have a good feeling, even though Muffins should be back in her apartment, hopefully regretting running away the day before.

Walter coughed, his throat rattling. "I saw him dashing down the road toward the Carlton's again."

"That's impossible," Holly stated. She'd locked the door this morning.

Walter held out his hands about twelve inches wide. "Oh, is he about this size? Gray? White nose?"

"Yes," Holly mumbled.

"Let's go. I'll give you a ride." Mason stood and tucked the newspaper under his arm.

ON THE DRIVE to Mason's home, latte clutched in her hand, Holly couldn't appreciate the passing scenic town. The words and not-so-subtle accusations of Millicent's article kept repeating in her mind. Wait until she got hold of her. Millicent would see that Holly was more than a weepy, suspicious newcomer to Fairview. And was what she said even legal? After she took care of Muffins, she'd head straight to the newspaper office and talk to the owner. Demand a retraction.

"Don't look now," Mason warned.

Too late. Holly focused as they passed *The Tasty Bite*. Customers flooded the shop, the line out the door, the parking lot jam-packed. Maybe Millicent was right. Holly was crazy to compete with another bakery in a town this size. This made her temperature grow hotter. If *Just Cheesecake* was doomed from the start, why write such horrible things?

"I told you not to look." He sped up so they left the shop behind. "Trust me. Don't focus on the competition. Focus on your own business and the goodwill you can spread to your customers."

"Easier said than done." Holly gaped as they pulled into the Carlton's driveway and approached the house. The size and detailed perfection still caught her off guard. "I can't believe this treasure is tucked away here."

Mason smiled. "I know. It's perfect. Right off Main Street but protected by trees. It's like we're in a different part of town instead of just miles from downtown."

They parked. A hired gardener or landscaper pruned the apple tree out front. A small gray dog yipped by his heels like they were good old buddies. Muffins!

"Looks like we solved one mystery." Mason glanced at his watch. "I'm expecting a conference call in a few minutes but feel free to grab something to drink from the kitchen."

Holly already had her hand on the door. "Thanks, that's a kind offer, but I have my own appointments to keep."

And a dog to murder! No more cheesecake scraps for him, left over from her kitchen experiments. No more allowing him to lick the bowl. No more doggie treats.

Mason headed inside. Holly marched across the lawn, a bit embarrassed that her dog was harassing someone doing his job. "Muffins. Come here."

Muffins continued to leap around the man, ignoring her completely. What had come over him? He always listened to her. He was trained to obey on command. Yet, he also had witnessed the murder and kept coming back here. Maybe he was trying to tell her something. Her attitude changed. This was an opportunity. Mason seemed nice, but she'd learned friendship was easy to fake. She straightened her scarf and studied the landscaper.

In the spring air, warming up fast, the man had broken a sweat, even in short sleeves. He was middle-aged with long black hair and a layer of scruff on his chin. He wielded the shears with ease, snapping at the branches.

"Excuse me!" Holly said.

Snap. Snap. Snap. The man kept attacking the tree, seemingly not hearing her.

"Excuse me!" she stated in a voice that was almost a yell.

He stopped and looked, dismissed her, and then kept at his job.

Holly inched closer, almost underneath him. "I'm terribly sorry to hear about your coworker, Ralph. Must be hard to work so soon after his death." The man kept working, so Holly kept talking. She ducked a falling branch. Investigating was dangerous work. "I didn't know Ralph, but I'm friends with Mason. I feel terrible, especially with his wife and kids."

The man paused, grimaced, and then cut off another branch.

"Must be hard to keep up morale, to keep working." Holly chewed her lip. This man was hard to crack. "Especially with this terrible shock." She kept rambling, hoping the man would eventually answer. Most men would do anything to put off a blabbering female.

Finally, he lowered the pruning shears. "Shock? Now I wouldn't say it was a shock. Ralph was asking for trouble."

Interesting. "Trouble?" Holly pressed, eager for information. If she knew more about Ralph, she could understand motive, then she could find the real murderer and clear her name and save her business. The fact that Muffins yipped and nipped at the man's pant leg encouraged her. He was acting out of character, because he wanted to help her. "Was he in some sort of trouble? Financial? Work?"

"Let's just say..." His words were drowned out by the squeal of tires as a yellow convertible screeched to a stop in the driveway.

"Yes?" Holly prodded, feeling the moment slipping away.

THE LANDSCAPER HAD stopped talking. In fact, he quit working and strode toward the house. Muffins lay at her feet. "Now you play the role of obedient dog. Figures."

A gorgeous blonde stepped from her car. Her heels were six inches and her dress flashed in the sunlight. The landscaper glanced back once more at Holly before disappearing around the side of the house.

"Oh, my gawd!" The woman strode across the yard, not wobbling a bit. "Is that the cutest dog I've ever seen, or what?"

That was debatable, thought Holly. Muffins responded right away, on his feet, tail wagging, tongue out.

The woman crouched, welcoming Muffins into her arms. "What a cutie, you are." She talked in a baby voice and held him like a baby. "Are you hungry? Do you need something to eat?"

He whimpered.

"Hi. I'm Holly."

The woman stopped cooing. Her eyes grazed Holly as the woman took in her humble outfit. "I'm Madeleine. Is this your dog?"

"Yes."

"Are you feeding him? Because he seems hungry."

"Yes. He's been fed. He ran away this morning." Somehow. Holly wanted to know how he escaped from the house after she'd locked the door.

Madeleine rubbed noses with Muffins. "Did you need a little adventure, you poor thing?" She addressed Holly. "You know, even small dogs need plenty of exercise. Many owners

75

think they can leave their dog inside all day. It's quite an injustice."

"I promise. He's had plenty of chances to stretch his legs." Holly redirected the conversation. "So, who was the worker?"

"Ralph? I think?" Madeleine paused, concentration etched on her face. She realized her blunder, her cheeks reddening. "I mean, not Ralph. That's impossible." She giggled and waved off her mistake, showing off her neon pink nails. "This man's name is...oh, I can't keep all the staff that come through here straight. Joe? Harry? I have no clue."

Holly was beginning to think she didn't have a clue about much. Madeleine must be Mason's sister. They were polar opposites. Still, this was opportunity. "Sorry to hear about Ralph's death. It must be hard on your family."

"It was dreadful. The poor guy." Her expression darkened. "And that new shop owner. Heather something. I can't believe she would accuse *The Tasty Bite* after killing a man."

Holly fumed. "Or maybe the reporter exaggerated the story."

Madeleine gasped. "Never! Millicent would never do such a thing." She narrowed in on Holly. "You look familiar. Do I know you?"

"Um, no. I'm friends with Mason. Just followed my rascal dog here." She opened her arms to receive Muffins from Madeleine, then she inched away, ready to make a break for it.

"Are you new in town?" Her eyes lit up. "You're Heather! What are you doing here? Coming back to take care of any remaining business?"

Muffins leaped from her arms and sprinted around the side of the house. This time Holly felt nothing but relief. "Sorry. Have to get my dog." She took off after Muffins, leaving Madeleine in shock. "And it's Holly," she shouted over her shoulder.

Behind the house, Holly stopped and stared. Unbelievable. That was another mystery solved. Muffins nibbled bacon treats from the landscaper's hand.

***

HOLLY DIDN'T BOTHER to ask Mason for a ride back to town. With Muffins by her side, she started the walk back.

"Good thing Mason doesn't live out in the boonies, right Muffins?" She glanced at her dog trotting along beside her. "So you decide to stick by me now. I see how it is. Well next time I might not come chasing after you."

And here Holly thought Muffins witnessed the crime and had been leading her to the killer by running to the Carltons. He'd been after the bacon treats. Enough about the Carltons. She had bigger issues.

Even though her rage at Millicent and the newspaper article had been delayed, it rose fresh in Holly's mind, the words like blinking neon signs. The whole town would think she was guilty! Muffins had been a distraction. The town would boycott *Just Cheesecake* unless she solved the mystery and cleared her name. Those thoughts careened in her head as she headed straight toward the newspaper office.

At the doors to the tiny office, Holly hesitated. She knew better than to go on a rampage, complaining and yelling. Even if the paper printed a retraction, the damage was done. The words couldn't be unread. After a few deep breaths and calming thoughts, she picked up Muffins and entered the office.

It was neat and tidy. A main desk sat unmanned but obviously meant for customers placing ads. A short hallway led to offices—Holly assumed for the editors and reporters. She should probably wait, but why not explore? Look around. Take a peek in the offices or at the names on the doors.

Feeling guilty, Holly crept past the main desk and down the hallway. The place seemed deserted. No muffled voices from behind the doors. They must all be to lunch, which made sense as Holly's stomach growled. What she needed was a sidekick to whistle when someone returned. She rubbed Muffins' head. She never could stay mad long at the pooch. "Sorry. I don't exactly trust you to stand guard. Not when you have the choice of bacon treats."

The second door had the name, Millicent Monroe, on it. Bingo!

Holly twisted the knob, glanced back to the front entrance, and then opened the door and slipped inside. Compared to the front desk, Millicent's office bloomed with color. Framed photos lined the windowsill. Large posters of cute kittens were on the wall. Again, Holly felt her stomach drop and the pain that comes from betrayal. There had been so much potential for friendship with Millicent. Holly had to laugh at some of the posters. A tiger kitten with the most mournful expression hung onto the edge of a couch. It read: Hang in There.

With a sigh, Holly shook it off. She didn't have much time to investigate. She went right to the desk and shuffled through the papers and notepads.

Millicent's illegible scribble covered most of the papers. Holly flipped through the notepad to a crossed-out, to-do list.

Make nice with the new girl?

Talk to Madeleine at breakfast about business.

Visit Officer Trinket.

Write one hell of an article!

Holly had a hard time looking away from the first point. The new girl must be her. She'd been trying to rationalize how Millicent was just writing the news. It was her job after all. Her efforts toward friendship, her welcoming words, might not have been a complete lie. But this blew that theory out of the bakery. Millicent had targeted Holly for her job. For the big article.

The door shut at the front. Voices entered, jabbering and laughing. Lunchtime was over. Panicked, Holly flipped faster. A few pages in—because Millicent seemed to have a list for everything—Holly came to a clean page with one word on it.

Ralph Newton.

Underneath was an address. Holly fumbled for her phone as the door opened to Millicent's office. Quickly, Holly flipped the notepad shut and sat in Millicent's chair. Like she'd been waiting for her all along. She stroked Muffin's back, feeling like quite the evil villain.

"You!" Millicent gasped, her face turning all sorts of shades of red.

"At least you have a conscience. That's good to know." Holly plastered on a smile.

"I see you managed to find some clothes today," Millicent shot back.

"Speaking of pajamas, I thought I might stop by and let you snap a few photos while I'm dressed. In case you want to write any more slander about me in the paper in the future."

Millicent smiled. "You're funny." Then she took on a cavalier attitude. "I would take you up on that, except the candids sell more copies. And in this digital world, I need all the help I can get. But maybe I can stop by for a photo shoot tomorrow morning. Any other cute PJs?"

Within the span of seconds, Holly contemplated her next move. She could rant and rave, but somehow, she had a gut feeling that would get her nowhere. Make her feel better? Sure. But she'd rather leave with a clue.

Millicent spoke first as if reading her mind. "Aren't you here to yell at me?"

Holly shrugged. "I thought about it, but then I realized you were doing your job. Why you came after me I don't know yet. But I'll figure it out. I also understand that incompetent reporters have to resort to pretending to be nice by welcoming strangers to town to find inspiration." Millicent clenched her fingers into fists, so Holly kept going. "When they can't find any real information by following clues, they have to create headlines out of nothing."

"That's not true. The body was found in your shop!" She pointed a finger at Holly.

"True." Holly picked up Millicent's notepad. She wanted a quick picture and then she could skedaddle. "Or you could have used clues you had. But maybe that would require getting off your duff or taking a break from mocha lattes and Danishes."

Millicent snarled. "That's mean."

"And what you wrote wasn't?" Holly accidentally dropped the notepad to the floor. She straightened out, leaving her arm by her side that had her phone ready to go. "I wanted to stop by and congratulate you on a shocking article. If you wanted people talking, it worked. And my suspicion of poor reporting was confirmed." Holly leaned over, placed Muffins on the floor, and snapped a picture of Ralph's address under Millicent's desk. "Sorry about that. Didn't mean to mess up your desk." She placed the notepad back. "I'll be going now."

Millicent stared, her mouth open, eyes narrowed. Of course, Muffins, the traitor, went right to her. Holly snatched him up on the way out. She couldn't help but leave Millicent with one last barb. "And thanks again for the welcome."

10

BACK AT HER apartment, Holly discovered the method of escape Muffins used. The window in her kitchen was open, the screen broken. She settled in on her love seat with a sandwich and cup of tea. She needed to cleanse her emotional palate after talking with Millicent and before she headed to Ralph Newton's. Hopefully, his family knew of any grudges or enemies Ralph had formed. She could leave with real clues to hand over to Officer Trinket.

And her good name and business could be cleared.

Muffins yipped and nipped at her ankles.

"Oh no, Mr. I-love-bacon. This time you're staying right here." She picked up Muffins and dropped him in her bedroom. "There you go. There's no way you can escape my bedroom, little Houdini."

Just to make sure, Holly grabbed a kitchen chair and stuck the top of the back under the doorknob. Her windows were locked. If Muffins escaped, then Holly would call in Millicent to report on a magic dog. Now that would be shocking news. Almost as shocking as murder.

With her phone and water bottle, Holly headed out. This time, she hopped in her junky four-door and spluttered to the outskirts of the town. She glanced at the address before pulling into a dirt driveway, number 41 Backwoods Lane. She shrugged off her nerves. Trees surrounded the expansive yard, not another driveway in sight. She guessed it really was backwoods in Fairview.

Her door creaked open. She almost wished she'd brought Muffins. Outside her car, she gave herself a pep talk. "Think of your business. Think of your dreams. Think of the newspaper article! Think of cheesecake. You can do this."

With her phone, she hoped to record some of the meeting, crucial evidence, something—anything—about why someone would want Ralph Newton gone.

She knocked. After a minute, she knocked again. "Hello?"

Holly had a choice. She could come back later, but what if Millicent arrived and got the scoop before her? Then the family might not be as willing to talk, especially on the heels of a reporter who made people nervous. Or, she could pretend the door was already open, and she thought she heard someone tell her to enter.

"What?" she called. "You want me to come on in? Oh, thanks!" Holly turned the knob, which wasn't locked, and pushed the door open.

Early afternoon shadows barely slipped through drawn shades and closed curtains, casting the room into murky darkness. Stumbling forward, stepping over beer cans and trash, Holly headed toward the mantle lined with framed photos. Where were Ralph's wife and family? Why was the place such a mess? She traced a finger through the dust on one of the pictures. Ralph with what appeared to be his wife and two kids. Holly studied the room: the couch, the lamps, the worn coffee table. Other than that, the room was pretty bare: not one feminine touch.

An uneasy chill whispered across her neck. The place felt empty, but it was more than that. Nothing added up. She picked through Ralph's things, looking for a clue of some kind. If Ralph was innocent, why had he sent his family away? If that's what he did. She swallowed another disturbing thought. Or maybe they had died, and this job was a fresh start for him. Maybe trouble had followed him to Fairview...and found him.

She spotted nothing in the small living room so moved toward the kitchen bathed in a soft light from the one window in the house with no shades. "Hello?" she called again, in case someone was home.

No answer.

She entered the kitchen and gasped. The worker from yesterday, the one who fed Muffins bacon treats was sleeping, his head on the table.

"Excuse me," she said softly.

She crept closer and this time couldn't shake the feeling of dread that fell over her. The man's arm dangled, his fingers grazing the cracked linoleum. His head lay at an odd angle. It was such an uncomfortable position to fall asleep, but maybe he was extremely tired. Maybe he'd been working double shifts. Why was he in Ralph's home? In his kitchen like he lived here?

Then Holly noticed the slice of cheesecake next to him. Half of it eaten. She flashed back to her own past. Anything was possible, even poison. Ralph, or this guy, didn't seem the type to splurge on cheesecake, and the rest of the cake sat on the counter, a card attached.

It drew her, like a magnet. She shuffled forward, her gaze zeroed in on the card and the plastic container. Both of which were familiar. She wanted to run away screaming, but she had to see with her own eyes what she already knew in her gut. What she feared.

Strawberries decorated the top corner of the card, the typing in an adorable curly Q font. The kind she loved and had chosen to brand her business.

Sorry for your loss. Prayers to you and your family.

Just Cheesecake

Holly gasped and almost crumbled on the spot.

"Hey, Holly!" someone called from the other side of the room.

As a knee jerk reaction, Holly looked. The light blinded her as the camera flashed.

"Thanks for the picture. This will go great with the shocking headline for tomorrow." Millicent whirled around and headed back toward the front door.

"Oh no, you don't!" Holly charged and tackled Millicent to the floor. "No way are you going to print that picture."

"Why not? Another cheesecake. Probably yours. Again." She grunted and tried to push Holly off her. "Obviously poisoned."

Millicent finally broke free and scrambled to the door. Holly caught her foot and hung on desperately. Millicent kicked several times but couldn't shake Holly. "Guess my article wasn't so crazy after all. You came to frost Ralph's friend. Permanently."

Anger surged. Managing to get to her knees, Holly tackled again. Millicent crashed into the front door, landing hard. "Unless my crazy theory has merit. That *The Tasty Bite* feels threatened and is framing me for murder."

"Enough," Millicent snarled and threw a punch.

It landed on Holly's face, stunning her for the moment. Another flash. Another cackle of glee.

"This will make an even better shot." She ran across the grass to her car parked behind Holly's. The engine roared, and Millicent zipped away.

Holly sat, stunned, staring across the room and into the kitchen. How did her cake get here? How did someone obtain the *Just Cheesecake* cards? They weren't even in the shop yet, but at her home on the kitchen counter. Her home. Someone must've broken in and stolen them. That's how Muffins escaped! He wasn't a Houdini after all.

Sirens sounded across town, drawing closer. Millicent must've put in the call. Instinct told Holly to run away and bring the evidence with her, but Millicent had it all on camera. No use running. It would make her look guilty, so she sat and waited. Curious, she decided to inspect the cheesecake. She sniffed it. She observed the texture, the look. It appeared fresh. Like someone had just baked it. She certainly hadn't done any baking.

The sirens were right outside Ralph's house before they shut off. Seconds later, the door burst open. Several uniformed men stampeded inside with guns.

"I'll take care of her," a familiar voice said. "Start breaking down the crime scene. Gather all the evidence." Officer Trinket's voice lowered. "Holly? I'm going to take a look in the kitchen. I'll be right back. Don't go anywhere."

Holly stared at the carpet, stained and torn. Shock rippled through her system. This couldn't be happening. She hadn't thought things could get worse than yesterday.

A minute later, Officer Trinket knelt next to her. "Holly? Your cheesecake is on the counter."

"It might be mine," Holly mumbled.

"The man who died ate a piece. It looks like poison, even though we won't know for sure until the lab results return."

"I know," Holly said.

"The man also worked for the Carltons."

"I know. I met him yesterday."

Officer Trinket sighed. "You know you should let the police do the investigating. Right?"

Holly didn't bother answering. She didn't have a choice but to find the killer. Her good name and her business were on the line.

"It looks like there was a struggle. Almost as if you stayed to make sure he died. And before he did, he fought you."

"Huh?" That didn't make sense. "I fought with Millicent."

"Millicent?" he questioned. "Millicent called to say you'd stolen information from her office. When she realized it was Ralph's address, she was worried about you so she called me."

"Oh, I'm sure she did."

"I hate to do this, but the evidence doesn't look good. I'm going to have to bring you down to the station."

His words sank in. "Y-you're going to arrest me."

His cheeks grew pink. "I wouldn't quite...well, yes."

11

AT THE STATION, in the interrogation room, Officer Trinket offered her a cup of coffee. "Want a week-old donut to go along with that?" he joked.

She barely smiled. How could she joke after the past few hours? But if he was joking that was a good sign, right? Time to get in a question or two. "You don't think I poisoned Ralph's friend...what was his name?"

"Joseph Carter. Here in town for some extra work. Or that's what he told the Carltons."

"Hmm." They were both friends. They both worked for the Carltons. They both died. Whatever Ralph knew, Joseph must have known too. "You realize that both the targets had absolutely no connection to me?"

He quirked an eyebrow. His sandy blond hair was in need of a cut. Longer strands fell across his forehead, making him look a lot younger. Almost like a teenager. Kinda cute, in his own way.

"No connection?" he asked. "You sure about that?"

Holly fought the blush rising in her cheeks. No connection other than Ralph's body showing up in her *Just Cheesecake* shop, and then, one of her cheesecakes being used to take out Joseph. "That's just cheesecake." She smiled at her joke, then said. "That has nothing to do with me. It would be easy to swipe the cards...easy to plant the body."

"Really? The murder happened in the shop. No trail or trace of any violence in the surrounding area."

"Well, you're a cop. Figure it out," she said then regretted it. "Sorry. I'm a little grumpy."

"That's okay. Where were you today before arriving at Joseph's house?"

"I had coffee with Mason in the cafe, realized Muffins had run away again, and found him at the Carltons where I met Joseph. Then I walked to town to confront Millicent on her slanderous article. Can you arrest her for that?"

"No." He cleared his throat, nervous. "Can anyone confirm your walk back to town, other than the Carltons?"

"No."

He leaned back in his chair and rubbed his chin. "I'll be honest. It doesn't look good. I think we're going to have to keep you overnight. We'll have the lab results in the morning."

"Overnight?" That was preposterous. What about Muffins? "Nothing's been proven. You can't do that."

Officer Trinket lost the friendly, casual look. "Oh, yes I can. And I will."

Later, locked in the small local cell, Holly fumed. He'd been so nice—why had she let her guard down? Cops couldn't always be trusted. Cops weren't always the good guys. Sometimes, they were tempted by greed and gave in to lining their pockets, trading in their decency, their honesty, their moral values. Why hadn't she demanded to see a lawyer?

She lay back on the hard bed, not wanting to look at the metal toilet in the corner. Someone broke into her house. Someone stole her cards. Someone stole one of her cheesecakes. She stubbornly refused the tears that wanted to fall. This was absolutely crazy. As she lay there, eyes closed, her thoughts wandered. She had a revelation, a glory hallelujah moment where the light broke through.

Just because one of her custom-designed cards was attached to the cake, didn't mean it was her cake.

***

THE NEXT MORNING, Holly rubbed her eyes but refused to stretch her sore back in front of Officer Trinket. "Best night's sleep ever," she stated as she marched from the cell.

"Really? Best night ever?"

"Yup." She headed straight toward the door, because if she stopped, even for one second, she'd probably give in to her tears. Her night had been terrible. She'd tossed and turned, racked by nightmares of giant cheesecakes smothering her. Several times, she'd shot up in the dark gasping for breath.

"Holly," Officer Trinket said.

She paused, hand on the door, not looking back. "What?"

His voice softened but still had a steel edge to it. "Lock your doors. Be smart and keep your focus where it belongs—in the kitchen...and be safe."

She widened her eyes. "I can do more than just sit in a kitchen. This isn't the 50s. If I knew your mama I'd be stopping by for tea to tell on you. She'd give you a slap upside the head."

"My mama?" He looked puzzled. "I didn't mean—"

"Too late. Too little." She closed the door then muttered a curse. When the door opened, she closed her eyes in humiliation but turned, bumping into Officer Trinket. He stood, her keys dangling from his fingers. "And, in case you're wondering, the cheesecake tested positive for poison, but we can't prove it was yours. Anyone could put a cheesecake in one of your containers."

She snatched them from him. "Thank you. I already knew that."

Halfway home, Holly felt bad. Office Trinket wasn't being sexist. He meant kitchen as in focus on her business. Still, she'd enjoyed giving him a hard time. But he was right about one thing. She did need to focus. Time to go where she'd never gone before.

Undercover.

At home, Holly picked up Muffins and apologized. She fed him, took him for a walk, and spent quality time snuggling on the couch. "Yeah, that's right. You know Mama loves you." She filled up a second bowl with dog food. "Here you go. Just in case I get thrown in jail again."

Holly rifled through her clothes for the perfect disguise. She had never been into *The Tasty Bite*, but her photo had been plastered all over the morning newspaper the day before. She stood in front of her now half-empty closet and tapped her chin. "Hmm." If people only knew her from her frog pajamas and possible murder rap, they wouldn't have any idea of her as a person. If she walked in sophisticated and elegant and suave, no one would even suspect she was Holly Hart: newcomer, brilliant creator of *Just Cheesecake*, murderer.

And a large, floppy hat that kept her face in shadows wouldn't hurt either.

After ten minutes of dressing, slipping into a pair of navy slacks and short heels--she didn't want to be too overdressed—she put on a cami and a tan button-up blouse. For the final touch, she placed her tan floppy beach hat over her red hair. Her hair! She twisted it into a bun and placed the hat over it. There. Perfect.

No one would recognize her.

Ten minutes later, she sat outside her competition, the possible company that framed her for murder to drive her out of town—and she wanted to throw up. It was almost blasphemous. For the first ever, she feared and felt sick about walking into a bakery. That thought pushed her over the edge. She mustered up some indignation. Her future was on the line!

Easy peasy. Walk in. Order a piece of cheesecake. Taste it and somehow compare it to the cheesecake locked away in evidence, being analyzed for poison. Of course, she should've snapped a photo of the cheesecake at the crime scene for comparison. Of course, she couldn't ignore the danger that if it was poisoned and she tasted it for comparison...she could die. She'd bake that muffin when she got there.

With a deep breath and more mental encouragement, Holly pushed the hat farther on her head and approached *The Tasty Bite*. She fell in love at first sight. The shop was adorable. She loved the post and beam structure that at one point must have been a house. It came with charm, antiquity, and a sense of belonging. The insides were just as wonderful. Soft pastels in warm colors—all psychologically proven to be more inviting to customers. The owner of *The Tasty Bite* not only had a sense of style but was smart too.

She took a seat in the corner and tried to look oblivious and innocent, just another customer.

So far so good.

From her spot, she observed the glass showcase filled with pastries, muffins, croissants, cookies...and cheesecake. Her gaze was drawn to the man standing behind the counter. Her sworn enemy if indeed he was behind all this.

The funny thing was that the more she studied him, the harder time she had finding those negative feelings. He looked like the great grandfather any kid would want. His bushy eyebrows overshadowed eyes beaming with kindness. He smiled and shared a nice word with every customer who approached the showcase. He knew every person by name. He laughed, a hearty, contagious chuckle. In fact, she stifled a smile. How could this man possibly have one evil bone in his body? Impossible.

Someone flopped into the seat next to her. "I know exactly what you're thinking. And you're right."

Charlene observed Holly with her shrewd gaze.

SO MUCH FOR being undercover. Holly narrowed her eyes at Charlene, throwing back at her the same knowing look. Charlene's hair still had that natural flyaway style, and a peek under the table told her Charlene must never take off the yellow boots. "Oh, and what was I thinking?"

"To start, you're wondering why I'm wearing these darn boots all over God's creation. Right now, it's none of your business, though. Every woman needs her secrets. But that's not what I was talking about." She closed her mouth and sat back in her seat, soaking in the suspense created by her unsaid thoughts.

"Fine." Holly sighed. "I'll play your little game. What was I thinking as you walked in?"

Charlene prolonged the suspense, rubbing her chin, still eyeing Holly. Finally, with a jolt, she was perched on the end of the chair. "I'd say, based on your ridiculous disguise, you're here on some sort of mission. Some undercover work, and you find that thrilling. Most likely you're someone who enjoys a good mystery. Am I wrong?"

"No," Holly said and puffed out her chest. "But my disguise is not—"

"And..." Charlene crooked her finger at Holly. "Since you have been accused in the papers of being the mysterious killer, you decided to clear your good name in hopes your business won't completely fail."

"Gee, thanks for the vote of confidence."

"Just saying it like it is." Charlene hesitated, leaning back once more in her chair. "I'm not sure you're emotionally capable of hearing the rest of my thoughts."

"I assure you,"—Holly straightened, rather miffed at Charlene's subtle, or maybe not so subtle, insult—"My emotional state is just fine." The words stumbled out though because if she were honest—she wasn't just fine. "Okay, well maybe if that lousy cop hadn't thrown me in jail overnight for no good reason since he couldn't see that logically if I were going to poison someone through cheesecake—why would I use my own cards and my cake? Though, I'm rather suspicious of the source of the cake."

"Exactly!" Charlene shouted. When she realized she had drawn attention, she lowered her voice. "Sorry about that. Wouldn't want anyone to see through your clever disguise."

"Again, with the disguise? I'll have you know that a lot of thought went into this outfit. The town expects some frivolous, stupid girl wearing frog pajamas." Holly swept her hand over her clothes. "I give them sophistication and elegance."

Charlene stated clearly, using exaggerated pronunciation, "Rules of going undercover. Never wear a trench coat and sunglasses."

"Obviously. I'm not, if you didn't notice."

"You might as well be though because you stick out. This town isn't about sophistication and elegance. It's about real people, doing real work, and living their lives. You might've hidden your red hair, but anyone could see through the flimsy disguise. I did."

Holly deflated. "You're probably right."

"Now, to let me complete my thoughts. You came in here wondering if the owner of *The Tasty Bite* possibly framed you. You're desperate. Especially after spending the night in a jail cell. Already knew about that." She tapped against her spring coat, causing the tip of the town paper to stick out from one of the inside pockets. "Except when you walked in and saw Pierre you knew a man who exuded that much kindness couldn't be a killer."

Holly's gaze wandered away from Charlene and to the glass showcase. Right now she could eat through the entire bottom level. At least the cookies. She returned her gaze to the town paper, realizing that if Charlene knew she spent the night in jail, she must've had a source. "Can I see your paper for a moment?"

"Nope." Charlene quickly closed the flap of her coat. "Buy your own."

"What if I buy you a piece of cheesecake? Then can I look at it?" Holly asked.

"A piece of cheesecake, huh?" Charlene mumbled to herself.

Holly finished Charlene's thought. "The killer could've used any cheesecake. Anybody could waltz in and buy one."

"Or they could have access to it." Charlene nodded toward the entrance.

Millicent Monroe flounced through the door, looking rather smug, a copy of the newspaper tucked under her arm. She didn't look around the place but went straight to the counter and talked with Pierre.

"She's the last person I want to see," Holly said.

"Don't blame you one bit. Keep watching though. Every day Pierre's daughter visits him. They chat. He gives her a blueberry muffin sprinkled with sugar. She gives him a kiss on the cheek."

"Pierre's daughter doesn't even know me. Millicent was the one who put those words in my mouth. I'd never truly thought another business owner would kill a man to get rid of the competition. She preyed on my moment of weakness. My shock at finding the body. My disappointment of a failed grand opening."

Millicent pointed out a muffin. Pierre chuckled and opened the glass case.

"All true," Charlene said. "But what if her father's business was her inheritance? The one thing that secured her future if she never made it as a novelist or a journalist."

Holly watched in amazement, her jaw slowly opening as Millicent reached across and pecked Pierre's cheek. Halfway toward the door, muffin in hand, she called out, "Goodbye Papa!"

"Why that conniving, no-good, rotten, moldy muffin. A blueberry one at that." Holly thought of all the ways Millicent had deceived her. When she planted the thought in her head the other day, Millicent failed to reveal that the owner of Holly's direct competition, *The Tasty Bite*, was none other than her father. "That teaches me a lesson. I thought a small town wouldn't have the lies and the fakery. Guess I was wrong."

"Don't let one rotten egg spoil the bunch," Charlene said.

"It's not just her. People in small towns are supposed to be honest and caring. Even Officer Trinket is running with the bad guys."

"Excuse me?" Charlene asked. "What do you mean?"

"I don't know for sure." Holly felt sheepish. "But the way he locked me up even after admitting I had no motive, told me he didn't want me sleuthing around. Maybe for him and his bank account the murder is best left unsolved."

"Are you sure it's not something else?" Charlene asked.

"Like what?"

"Maybe someone has a little crush. Officer Trinket is a hottie, don't you think?"

Again with the hottie? Holly had given no hint of a crush. She'd complained about him! It was almost as if Charlene was encouraging her to like Officer Trinket. "He's young enough to be your son."

Charlene laughed. "A woman at any age can appreciate good looks. So, do you like him?"

Officer Trinket? He was on the good-looking side. Not in a groomed Mason-Carlton-kind-of-way. But in the innocent-small-town-boy-kind-of-way.

"I can see it on your face. You like him!"

"That look was indigestion caused by my stay at the police station and his sexist remarks that I belonged in the kitchen." Holly left out that later she'd realized he meant to focus on her cheesecakes. She narrowed in on the paper again. "So, do we have a deal?"

"A slice of cheesecake for my copy of the paper?"

Holly nodded.

"Deal." Charlene rubbed her hands together. "I love Pierre's cheesecake." She added, "If you wanted competition, you got it. And maybe later I'll even teach you a thing or two about disguises and undercover work."

"Thanks," Holly said dryly. She went up and purchased two slices, her head down, slightly ashamed at her deception. She returned to the corner table.

Charlene slid the town paper across the table. "I have two thoughts. One, you should attend our mystery book club tonight. You might learn something. And two, maybe you should be using your feminine charm to do some sleuthing on that one."

Holly followed Charlene's gaze to the entrance. Mason Carlton had walked through the door.

13

MASON STRODE TO the counter, confident, every movement filled with the ease that comes from a life of money. Holly would recognize it anywhere.

From under her hat, she observed as he ordered a cinnamon muffin and chatted with Pierre in a calm, aloof manner. The scent of strawberries and cinnamon from her purchase wafted up. She was dying to try her competitor's cheesecake, but she hesitated. What if it was so divine, such a luxurious taste and texture that she could never compete? What if this one taste put her on a downward cycle of discouragement that affected her ability to create in the kitchen?

Charlene rapped her knuckles on the table. "Chin up, girl. It's just cheesecake." She smiled at her own play on words. She glanced at Mason. "Don't let your emotional involvement in this case affect your logic. You're not the only suspect here." Then, without even taking a bite, she picked up her dessert. "My cats love Pierre's cheesecake." She winked. "See you tonight at book club. My house."

She was left alone with Pierre's cheesecake.

Determined to get a taste, if only for the sake of the murder case, and the most recent murder, she sank her fork into it. After a moment of hesitation, she closed her eyes to block out the other senses—which was, after all, the best way to enjoy any pastry—and took the bite.

Heaven. The angels sang. The skies opened up. Holly let the taste swirl in her mouth. This was the best cheesecake she'd tasted.

Except her own, of course.

"Holly?" Mason asked.

She lowered her head. Maybe he'd walk on by. Hopefully, Pierre wasn't paying attention. Acting like she didn't hear him, she picked up her town paper and cheesecake and rushed outside.

Mason followed. "Holly? Is that you?"

Perhaps Charlene was right about her ability to dress in disguise and go undercover. Slowly, she turned and plastered on a smile. "Oh, Mason. Hello. Did you say my name?"

The corners of his mouth turned up, like he saw through her act. "I thought that was you. I almost didn't recognize you without your pajamas on."

Holly tried not to scowl. She had no desire to relive that day.

"Sorry," he said. "Just trying to make you laugh. I won't mention the pajamas again." He took in her clothing, her fancy choice of outfit, for a trip for cheesecake.

She knew exactly what message that sent. That she had money, too. Little did he know she'd left all that behind when she moved to Fairview. This was one of the few remaining outfits she'd brought with her. Just in case.

"Nice hat. But don't worry, I understand."

Panic seized her. "What do you think you understand?" How much did he know? He must've read the paper. He must suspect that her cheesecake was used in murder and that now, she would be the town outcast.

"Calm down. I only meant that obviously you're checking out the competition. Smart."

Holly deflated. She really was terrible with disguises. He saw right through her. A five-year-old probably could.

He laughed. "Oh, don't worry about it. Every business should check out what their competition is offering and what decisions they're making. In bigger business it's called corporate espionage."

She sank onto a nearby bench that lined the sidewalk. "I was that obvious?"

"Nah." He waved her off and sat next to her. "I have an eye for that sort of thing." He laughed. "Okay, well maybe a little."

"Great. But it's more than that." As the words formed, Holly decided to take Charlene's advice to do a little subtle investigating. "If you haven't read the town gossip, supposedly my cheesecake was used in the most recent murder of your employee. Another one."

"Ah, yes. I happened to read it. Very unfortunate."

"And very unfortunate that my cheesecake and my shop were used to throw the police off the trail of the real criminal."

Mason's forehead creased in thought. "It does seem odd that they would target you. Or maybe it's coincidence. I can recommend a good lawyer if you need one. You do have a lawyer, right?"

"Well, no. I'm innocent."

"That's not what matters. All they need is evidence and—"

"And a motive. Which I don't have. I didn't know Ralph or Joseph." She took a deep breath and went out on a limb. "But they did work for you. Do you have a lawyer?"

He burst out laughing. "You're adorable. Of course my family is suspect. As I told Officer Trinket. Our family hired these men to help them out. They came to us with the plea of needing a job to pay off debt collectors. And, well, we wanted to help them out." He stood. "But let's take a walk and chat about more pleasant topics."

Classic redirection, she thought. Maybe Mason had something to hide. Holly stuck the newspaper under her arm and tossed the cheesecake. She'd accomplished her mission and didn't need the extra calories. Though, it felt like a sin to throw away something so divine. So heavenly.

They walked away from *The Tasty Bite* and headed toward the main part of town, and toward *Just Cheesecake*.

The picturesque view took her breath away. The tree-lined street, cute shops and boutiques, the budding of trees soon to be in full blossom. Spring was on the way. Once again, Holly felt the burning desire for a fresh start—the whole reason she moved to Fairview. She couldn't let anything get in the way.

"I know the first few days have been rough, but overall, do you like Fairview?" Mason asked. He stuck his hands in his pockets, carefree and enjoying the nice weather.

Or pretending to.

"Other than running around in my pajamas, being seen by the entire town, embarrassing myself in front of a cute guy, and spending a night in jail, I'd say I'm loving small town life."

Mason cringed. "That bad, huh? There must be some positives in it all."

"Yes. Lots of positives. I love the charm of Fairview. The shops."

"Wait a second." Mason stopped walking. "Did you say a cute guy?"

She smiled mysteriously. "Why yes, I did. I just didn't mention the name of said cute guy."

"Oh." He acted properly humbled. "What attracted you to Fairview?"

The answer came immediately. "The feel of the town. I fell in love the minute I drove through."

"I agree. Fairview is my getaway, an escape from the stress of the corporate world. I do most of my work from home."

"And your father or boss doesn't mind that?" she asked, curious.

"Oh no. He definitely minds, but it was my decision."

Holly noted his determination, the steely glint in his eye. Mason had a side to him, the dangerous instinct of a shark that probably only came out during business hours. Was he determined enough to murder? And frame a newcomer to town?

She cleared her throat. "Enough about me. Just as you saw through my disguise, I saw through your attempt earlier to steer our conversation in a different direction." Not wanting to get too serious or too confrontational, Holly forced a smile and leapt into the role-playing. "Mr. Carlton, we have a serious dilemma here. Two of your employees have been murdered." She stuck out her thumb as if it was a microphone and she was the pesky reporter. "Do you have an alibi for this morning?"

He laughed a little too hard and a little too long. He coughed and straightened up, switching from casual to formal. "Why, in fact, I do. I was in the middle of a conference call. And how about that? Here comes my lawyer right now."

Walter Huffly strode down the street, slightly puffing. His bushy white hair seemed rather askew, his clothes rumpled. "Mason. There you are." He stopped to catch his breath.

Holly stuck out her mic with a smile. "And yes, Mr. Huffly, as Mason's lawyer can you confirm his alibi this morning. Was he, indeed, on a conference call?"

Huffly eyed the situation and smiled. "Yes, he was." He flashed her an apologetic look. "Lovely sense of humor. I see why Mason's taken a fancy to you, but I'm going to have to pull him away. Business."

Mason took her hand. "We'll finish the interview another time."

"Sorry about that," Huffly said. "Why don't you attend our dinner party tomorrow evening? Nothing fancy. Business casual."

Mason lit up. "Of course! Why didn't I think of that? Will you come? Tomorrow night?"

"I'd love to."

Walter Huffly and Mason strode back toward *The Tasty Bite*. Holly watched, pensive. He'd been a master at playing the game while not giving anything away. Maybe this dinner invitation was a godsend.

***

BACK AT HOME Holly flopped on the couch with a chicken salad wrap. Muffins snuggled on her lap. "What a morning."

The town paper lay on the cushion next to her. Her morbid curiosity pushed her to read it. Yet, she knew what the headline would hold. Another amazing article by the talented Millicent Monroe where she presented a skewed version of the truth.

After finishing her lunch, she couldn't handle the feeling of dread. Gently, she nudged Muffins off her lap and picked up the paper.

On the front page was a picture from the day before, of her in Joseph's kitchen. With a shocked and guilty look on her face, Holly was bent over the cheesecake. Her store's cheesecake. Or that was how it appeared. She groaned. "Great." It only got worse.

Another Day...Another Murder

It's not looking good for newcomer Holly Hart. After being captured in the act of trying to cover up her crime, Ms. Hart spent the night in jail. So far, she's the number one suspect. First, the body of Ralph Newton was found in her shop. Then, Ms. Hart was found with the body of Joseph. Officer Trinket refrained from comment.

Time of death is still to be determined and so is the method, but it appears that the cheesecake from Just Cheesecake contained poison. Joseph didn't have a chance.

Justice must be sought. We strongly encourage and support the police in their ongoing effort to rid our small town of a murderer.

If you have any information or photos, please contact our office.

Holly threw the paper across the room. She couldn't believe this trash passed as reporting. No mention of the connection with the Carltons. No mention that she had absolutely no motive. And, of course, no mention that the author of the article had a reason for Holly Hart to disappear. Permanently.

Someone knocked on the door, sharp and quick. "Holly? This is Officer Trinket. Open up."

OFFICER TRINKET KNOCKED again.

Holly clutched Muffins to her chest. "What should I do?" she whispered. Her night in jail, the darkness and the loneliness, flashed in her memory. Even though she'd survived, it wasn't something she wanted to experience again. "What if they found more evidence against me? What if that nasty bit of reporting influenced him?"

"I know you're in there, Holly."

"I'm not here," she called.

"Holly. We need to talk," Officer Trinket said in exasperation.

"Well, I'm napping. Make an appointment with my secretary."

"You don't have a secretary."

"Then come back tomorrow."

"Can you stop acting like a child and open the door?" he asked.

Holly huffed. Acting like a child? She strode to the door but left it closed. "I'm not the one who made an arrest and threw an innocent woman in jail. For the night, I might add. I'm not the one influenced by the lies of the media. I'm not the one consorting with the real criminals while my bank account grows nice and fat. I'm—"

"Did you accuse me of being a dirty cop?" His voice grew louder. "Since when do you get off accusing me of crossing the line?"

"I think it's rather fair. You accuse me of murder. I accuse you of playing dirty. What goes around comes around." She leaned her back against the door.

On the other side, he let out a sigh. "Holly." When he spoke his voice was soft, almost pleading. Vulnerable. "I have news...and I came to explain and apologize."

She turned and whipped the door open, her eyes narrowed. "Why should I trust you?"

He held up a coffee and a bag of donuts. "Because I come offering gifts?"

"Are those from *The Tasty Bite*?"

He nodded. "Yes."

"You sure they aren't poisoned?"

"Why would they be?"

"Because they want to run me out of town. That's why." She opened the door further. "You might as well come in."

Officer Trinket entered, handing her the coffee. They moved to her kitchen and sat at the table-for-two. Holly held the cup between her hands, soaking in the warmth. She almost wanted to smile. Trinket fidgeted with his cup, like he wanted to say something but didn't know how to say it.

"Why don't I start with evidence you might've overlooked?" She sipped her coffee and eyed the donuts.

First she needed to lay out her theory. "Millicent Monroe, in trying to protect her dad's business, has snapped my pictures and written articles that are supposed to pass for news. She has taken events out of context, twisted them to suit her purposes, which is to ruin my business before I've had a chance to even open my doors."

"That might be true. But is that a motive for murder?" He took a bite of a chocolate donut with sprinkles.

"More of a motive than I have, and I spent the night in jail."

"The body was found in your shop. Your footprints were in the frosting. A cheesecake that appeared to be from your shop was poisoned and the direct cause of someone's death. You were found at the scene of the crime. Your fingerprints were on the knife."

"But what motive do I have? I'm new in town." She stood and paced. "And did you ever think that someone is setting me up? Framing me for murder? Muffins went missing the other morning. Dogs can't unlock doors. Someone entered and stole my cards. They could have purchased a cheesecake from *The Tasty Bite* and passed it off as one of mine."

"Okay, okay. I agree. You don't appear to have a motive. If you'll give me a chance, I'll explain." He stopped fidgeting and straightened. "I take my duty to serve and protect the people of Fairview seriously. No, I don't think you had anything to do with those murders. I might have ideas and theories. I wanted whoever did this to think I had my sight on you, hoping they'd get sloppy, relax. I wanted them to think their plans to frame you were working. Those articles helped my case."

"That wasn't a reason to put me in jail."

Officer Trinket looked down, his cheeks reddening. "Sorry about that." He looked her in the eye. "But I'd do it again if I had to. You need to stop nosing around in this case."

"Apology not accepted. Unless...." she teased.

"Unless what?"

"I know how to clear my name. I tasted a cheesecake from *The Tasty Bite*. Let me taste the cheesecake delivered to Joseph and I'll tell you in three seconds whether that cake is mine or not."

"Absolutely not!" The words exploded from his mouth. "It was poisoned."

"I could take a quick bite. Just one. That's all I'd need. You could keep a close eye on me."

"Never. That's not an option. We could do a forensic comparison if I felt that would lead to a substantial clue. Who baked the cheesecake isn't an indication of guilt."

"Exactly!" Holly cried. "I never should've spent the night in jail."

He raised an eyebrow. "You were at the scene of the crime?"

"Fine." Holly leaned back in her chair. She gazed out the window that looked over the street and her shop. The afternoon sun glinted off windows and cast a romantic glow. A tug of sadness fell over her at her failed grand opening. "What about the Carltons?"

"This case is none of your business."

"I'd say it is, considering my future depends on the real killer being caught."

"Let the police do their work," he said through clenched teeth. "Or by golly I will put you in jail another night for interfering with police work."

"Go ahead and try." Holly pushed the plate of donuts away. "I see this gift as the bribe it is. You might be able to sweet talk women with donuts, but not this one." She walked to the door and opened it. "You may leave now."

He walked over to her. "I mean it, Holly. Stay out of it."

She pointed to the hallway. "Leave."

"Fine."

"Fine."

After he left, she slammed the door.

"We're done investigating your shop. You're cleared for business." He stated this last piece, the news he came to share.

"Oh yeah," she called. "Like anyone's going to want to patronize my shop now."

She slid down the door until she was sitting on the floor. Muffins padded over and whimpered. "I know, little buddy. I was a jerk. You don't have to tell me that. I can't stand to see anyone get away with murder."

***

IT DIDN'T TAKE long for Officer Trinket's words to sink in. Holly's shop had been cleared! She could plan another grand opening. Bigger and better than the last one. She squeezed Muffins, unable to contain her joy.

She jumped up and grabbed her secret recipe book she'd stashed on top of the fridge. Thank goodness she'd hidden it. If it had been Millicent who broke in and stole her business cards, she would've swiped that too. First, Holly would run over to the shop, kiss its floor, then whip up some mini-cheesecakes for the mystery book club.

At her shop, Holly dove into the baking process. She also needed to make a big batch of the cheesecake filler to freeze. She'd create a new and improved creation to show off for the opening. Something like Sweet Addiction. Maybe a cheesecake brownie. Her new opening sign could say, "What's your poison?"

Or maybe not. Laughter bubbled up.

After kissing the freezer bags filled with her secret recipe, developed from months of experimenting in her mother's kitchen, she set to work on the mini-cheesecakes for this evening.

Several hours passed before she exited her kitchen. Exhausted but happy and relaxed from baking, she waltzed across the floor. Time for book club where Charlene and her friends would be the first in town to taste her cheesecake. Maybe they'd spread the word. Generate a little business.

Locking up at her shop and double-checking, Holly nodded with satisfaction at the newly replaced locks. She paused in the parking lot, content, as she stared across at her cozy apartment. For the first time in several days, she felt hope.

A shadow passed in front of the window.

Holly peered carefully. In her excitement, had she left the light on? Who was in her house?

FOR A PARALYZING second, Holly couldn't move, stunned, shocked beyond all belief. Did she need to put a steel barricade in front of her door to keep out intruders? She'd have to talk to her landlord.

The light clicked off in her kitchen. This person had some nerve. It could be Millicent. But what did she have to gain? She already had spread enough slander through her articles that it would take Holly a good long while with lots of free samplers and half-off sales to get *Just Cheesecake* off the ground. If it wasn't Millicent, it had to be the real killer, possibly planting evidence.

Holly had come too far to sit by and watch someone destroy her future. She should call Officer Trinket or 911. She should call Charlene, so someone could testify that Holly wasn't imagining the intruder. But the door opened, and a bundled figure stepped onto her deck and made its way down the stairs.

"Hey!" Holly yelled. Her momentary paralysis over, she took off across the parking lot and the street. "You were in my house. I see you!"

The figure stopped and then raced down the wooden steps. The coming dark obscured the person enough that Holly couldn't recognize him or her.

She ran faster, pushed harder. Enough was enough. As she crossed the street, the figure disappeared around the corner of the house. Out of breath, adrenaline running, Holly sprinted around to the back of her apartment building.

Nothing. No one.

The person had disappeared. There was nothing but forgotten rose bushes in the small yard. Except...for an almost invisible path, dirty and overgrown, that led into the woods backing up her place.

"No time like the present." Holly had meant to explore these woods.

It was late enough in the afternoon that as soon as she stepped a few feet onto the path, the light dimmed. Dark roots twisted, like arthritic hands, over the path. Overgrown bushes offered plenty of places to hide, and the skinny trees, all fighting for sunlight, had spindly, finger-like branches blocking her way.

She pushed through, ignoring the branches.

Finally, she stopped, listening. She was crashing through here like a herd of elephants. Her intruder would be making noise too.

She waited. Her breath was one of the few sounds, along with the creaking of the trees higher in the wind.

The loud crack of a branch breaking sounded off to the right. Ignoring all the fairy tales rules to never stray from the path, Holly forged through the brush, holding her arm out to bear the brunt of the sting of branches and thorns. The pain and scrapes would be worth it.

The farther she ran into the woods, the less effective she felt. She'd imagined tackling the intruder, and after a short struggle, in which she would be the victor, she'd call Officer Trinket. The murderer would be subdued underneath her, spilling out his testimony as she caught it on her phone, and her name would be cleared. Mystery solved. She'd be the hero, and on her grand opening, the townspeople would flock to her shop to buy her cheesecake.

This fantasy faded fast as the woods grew darker. She stopped to listen again, but the intruder seemed to have disappeared. Or, they knew these woods and the intertwining trails better than she did.

Forced to admit defeat, Holly headed back toward the path. Except that the overgrown trail never appeared. Refusing to let panic set in, she pushed through. It had to be somewhere. She dabbed at her cheek. Her finger came back with a bit of blood. The sting of cuts and scrapes brought tears of frustration. Maybe it had been a mistake to settle in this town. Surely, the signs were against her.

She moved slower, trudging through the dark. When she was at her wits end, ready to build a shelter and camp out for the night, she saw a metallic flash through the trees. A car! Civilization!

Only ten yards away was the road. She mustered up the energy for this final push and came out on a side road that connected with Main Street. She started the slow shuffle back, ready for a hot shower and lemon tea. And then to bed.

As much as she wanted to attend the book club, her enthusiasm had dwindled significantly.

Back at her apartment, Holly climbed the steps.

"About time you showed up," a crackly, familiar voice stated.

Holly startled and peered closer at the flyaway hair and the yellow rubbers. She felt the momentary relief of seeing a familiar face.

"What happened to you?" Charlene eyed Holly's face, no doubt noticing the angry red scrapes.

"I enjoyed a nice jaunt through the woods. I assume you're here for a purpose. Would you like some tea?" She could at least send the mini-cheesecakes with Charlene to the book club.

"Sure I would, but we can't dally long." She tapped the clunky watch on her wrist. "Book club will be starting soon, and I'm the host this week."

Holly didn't have to unlock her door. It stood slightly ajar. Muffins whimpered on the other side. Muffins! Holly burst through and picked up her little dog. "Are you okay, buddy? Surprised you didn't run away again." When she knew for sure that Muffins hadn't been hurt, she let the squirming dog back on the floor, and then placed the kettle on the stovetop and turned it on.

"You might want to go clean up. Not that I mind that you look like a wood elf, and the other ladies won't mind either. I thought you might."

Holly slowly let out a long stream of air. She couldn't keep lying. "Charlene?"

"Nope." Charlene held out her hand. "I don't want to hear it. No excuses. That's why I'm here. I thought you might try to back out of book club."

"You don't understand."

"We all have tough days. This book club is more than a social gathering. It's a commitment. Ups and downs will come. The last thing anyone should do is wither away at home feeling sorry for herself."

The kettle whistled. Holly poured two mugs of tea and plopped in the tea bags. Mentally exhausted, she slumped in a kitchen chair. "Here you go."

Charlene sat across from her, exactly where Officer Trinket sat earlier. The events of the day swirled in Holly's mind, causing nothing but confusion. Maybe a night filled with frivolous talk of murder would be good. Tomorrow morning, the answers would come.

"It doesn't matter if you read the book or not. This time. I invited a guest speaker."

"Really?" Holly perked up. This meant she could attend and not engage. She could sit back, eat tasty desserts, and be distracted for a good hour or so.

"Of course, in the future, there's a punishment for not reading the book."

Holly noticed the twinkle in Charlene's eye and teased back. "Maybe this club isn't for me."

"Oh, I think it is. Now slurp down your tea and go wash up. Time is tick-tocking past."

Holly carried her tea back to her bedroom. She needed a complete change of clothes. She felt sweaty and grimy after her fruitless tromp. Quickly, she jumped in the shower and gently washed her face. After she was dressed in skinny jeans and a red long-sleeved shirt, she dabbed on makeup, trying to hide the scrapes and the light bruise from her fight with Millicent.

Walking into the kitchen, she stated, "Well, what are you waiting for?"

***

CHARLENE LIVED ABOUT ten minutes from the center of town, on a winding road lined with budding trees that in the fall, with the colors, would be gorgeous. At the end of the driveway sat a log cabin with a front porch.

"I love it!" Holly said, the tray of mini-cheesecakes in her lap.

"I do too. Don't know why I leave it as often as I do." She parked and turned off the car. "Time to meet the ladies."

As Holly climbed the few steps to the porch, her enthusiasm grew. Clean and showered, the stress of the day fell away. After all, this was a great way to meet some of the ladies in town. And tonight? She'd relax and enjoy herself. Forget about the murders, except for the fictional ones.

Charlene led the way into her home. The cackle of laughter floated out from the living room. They sounded like a fun bunch even if murder was no laughing matter. Holly loved murder mystery jokes.

Holly almost bumped into Charlene at the entrance to the room. It was filled with knickknacks and afghans draped over brown leather couches—an antique-lover's dream. Holly loved the cozy feel, the soft lighting, the paintings of the countryside on the wall, along with family photos.

"What did you say you were doing in the woods?" Charlene whispered.

Holly bit her lip. She hated lying. "I didn't tell you the whole truth, but I'll fill you in later. It's not important now."

What had the intruder wanted?

They entered the room. Holly took in the women, most of them Charlene's age. Their weathered, lines faces were friendly and open. This might work out.

Her gaze fell upon a younger woman, more her age. Her blonde pixie cut fell across her face as she chatted with the woman next to her.

She had two red scrapes across her cheeks, also not well hidden by makeup.

16

HOLLY STIFLED A small gasp. Millicent? And the scrapes on her face were full-proof evidence of who'd been nosing around in Holly's apartment earlier. Right there, Holly wanted to charge across the room and tackle Millicent to the floor.

Charlene gripped Holly's arm and spoke soft and low. "Not here. Not now." She waltzed into the center of the room, dragging Holly with her. "And look who I brought? Someone who loves a mystery as much as we do."

All conversation stopped, as the group stared at Holly, from their seats on a couch, armchair, or kitchen chair pulled into the room. Their gazes dropped to the scrape and bruise on her cheek and then looked to Millicent's matching one. A few of them stuttered out the start of a hello, but somehow, the welcomes died.

"Goodness," Charlene exclaimed. "It's like you've all been invaded by aliens. Is this how we greet a guest?"

A chorus rose, of welcomes and hellos. A couple of the women, close to Charlene in age, stood and walked over.

One lady with streaks of purple in her hair held out her hand. "Surprised Charlie here didn't frighten you away. Don't you mind her crotchety way."

"Holly. Meet Kitty." Charlene leaned in toward Holly. "She's prone to exaggeration. Don't take much stock in what she says."

Kitty held up her finger. "I heard that." She leaned in close too. "If she gives you a hard time just threaten her cats. That'll get her in line. Works every time."

Charlene whacked Kitty in the arm. "There she goes again." Charlene grabbed the tray of mini-cheesecakes from Holly and shoved them at Kitty. "Go put these on the table before I kick you out of the club.

"I'm one of the founders. Impossible!" She huffed but took the tray and headed back toward the group.

Another lady, small in stature, with twitchy lips, smiled and waved.

"This here's Ann. She doesn't talk much. She's a good one to tell all your secrets to."

"Nice to meet you, Ann." Holly spoke to the larger group. "Nice to meet all of you."

Everyone settled in their seats and Holly was able to look at the whole group. Madeleine, Mason's sister, sat next to Millicent, and they were like two chipmunks, chattering away. Millicent bit her pinky fingernail. Classic guilt.

"Ooo! Dessert," Madeleine squeaked. "Hi, there, Holly. Whatever did you make? Looks scrumptious."

"Mini-cheesecakes. My secret recipe. A small preview of what's to come when my shop opens." Holly smiled, proud of her work. When there were several nervous smiles, she scanned the coffee table and noticed a large chocolate chip cheesecake. She forced a laugh. "Looks like I offered the bite-size version."

She didn't need to ask who brought the large cheesecake. The smug smile on Millicent's face spoke volumes. Not knowing whether to feel embarrassed or angry, Holly found a seat on the fringe of the circle. Charlene plopped down next to her.

Millicent swaggered to the table and cut a thick slice of cheesecake, then she walked toward Holly. "Here you go. Welcome to the club."

Gritting her teeth, Holly accepted the plate. Her body tensed when Millicent didn't return the motion by picking up one of her mini-cheesecakes. As the ladies watched, almost as if she were being tested on her good sportsmanship, Holly took a bite. "Excellent," she said through a mouthful, knowing she'd have to eat the whole darn thing.

"So where's the guest speaker and who is it?" Kitty demanded.

Holly had a feeling Kitty was a good a match for Charlene with her wit and fast thinking. She took another bite of cheesecake, her stomach churning.

"Oh, wait," Kitty said. "Let me guess. You roped your son into talking to a bunch of middle-aged women again."

"Middle-aged." Madeleine huffed. "Speak for yourself."

Charlene had a son? She hadn't mentioned a thing about that over the past two days. Not that Holly had asked either.

The *whoop whoop* of the siren sounded outside. "And there he is now, showing off as usual."

A minute later, the door opened. Officer Trinket walked through in full uniform. Her mouth slightly ajar, Holly's gaze darted between Officer Trinket and Charlene, whose whole face lit up as she beamed with pride.

Trinket, with his hands on his holster, walked into the room, eyeing the ladies. Holly remembered their earlier encounter, the donut bribe to encourage her to back off from the case, her night in jail with no explanation.

"What? No donuts?" Holly exclaimed. "I thought a cop would at least bring donuts."

Several of the ladies tittered. Charlene gave her a curious look, then dove into introductions. "Everyone knows my son, Trent. I invited him to talk about guilt and motives when it comes to murder."

Everyone murmured. Millicent whipped out her notebook, and Holly remembered she liked writing mystery stories. Probably why she felt at liberty to break into other people's apartments—in the name of research.

"Think I'll grab myself a cup of coffee before I get started, ladies." He sauntered into the kitchen like he was familiar with the place, which, of course, he was. A few seconds, he returned, dragging in another kitchen chair. He sipped the coffee. "Alright, motive. If you want to solve the murder mystery that you're reading"—he put special emphasis on the last two words—"you have to look at who has secrets, who has something to hide."

"Usually all suspects do," Millicent chipped in.

"You're right. So it's your job to study their body language and listen to what they say and how they say it."

Holly stepped in. "Let's say someone is really sweet and nice to a person—in the story, of course—and then turns out to have a hidden agenda, possibly connected to the murder. That agenda would be motive. Right?"

"Definitely," Officer Trinket said.

Holly stood, unable to contain the restlessness and the adrenaline that raced through her as she laced her words with accusation. "So what would it take, oh, let's say, for this person to spend a night in the town jail? How about breaking and entering into someone's apartment?"

Officer Trinket's ears turned a nice shade of red as he caught on that Holly was no longer talking figuratively. "It all depends on—"

"On what? Whether the cop had eggs or cereal for breakfast? Whether it rained on Tuesday that week?"

Trinket shifted as did a lot of the women who'd picked up on the under current of tension. Holly studied Millicent, who scribbled furiously in her notebook. Her archenemy would most likely play innocent, unless...Holly shocked her, said something so unexpected that Millicent would slip up.

Charlene interrupted Holly's train of thought. "Why don't we let Officer Trinket finish his thoughts."

All the women murmured in agreement.

"So as I was saying, an officer must have the training to pick out motive and follow through with an investigation. That's why detectives should be allowed to do their job without the interference of local amateur sleuths."

Charlene huffed. Holly realized that Charlene must stick her nose into his cases, too. Just like she did that day of Ralph's murder by keeping her in one place after she called her son, the cop. Holly was growing impatient. Time to step it up.

Holly walked toward the coffee table and picked up the chocolate chip cheesecake. "Let's say, that someone uses an everyday object, like a cheesecake,"—she made a sudden jab toward Millicent with the cake, who squealed and clutched Madeleine—"to either murder someone by asphyxiation or poison. Nothing a little arsenic won't kill, right?" Holly laughed. Even though it sounded more like a cackle, and even though she knew she should stop—she couldn't.

"Holly?" Charlene asked, her forehead knitted with worry.

A storm cloud crossed Millicent's face. She gripped her notebook so hard the page was tearing.

"Let's say, that this someone—completely fictional, of course—is not a murderer. Everyone knows it." Holly walked closer to Trinket. "And the local cop finds her pretty so ignores the outstanding evidence." Her voice grew louder, even though everyone was staring, hooked on every word. "What if this sweet, innocent person is covering for someone she loved dearly? Like her father?"

"That's crazy!" Millicent shot up from her seat, trembling. "My father wouldn't hurt a flea."

"So you're saying that you committed murder to make sure your father's business has no competition?" Holly accused. Even as the words left her mouth though, she knew she was wrong. Millicent didn't seem like a killer. An annoyance? Yes. But not a killer.

"That's it." Millicent picked up several of the tiny cheesecakes. "You've gone too far." She squeezed the cakes in her fist. "We don't need murder to stay in business. You'll be lucky to survive a year with your imitation cheesecake. My dad has worked years perfecting his recipes. No one can compete. No one!"

The cheesecake Holly had slaved over, oozed through Millicent's fingers. Even though Charlene spoke right next to her. Even though all the women were murmuring now, their voices rising in a cacophony of excitement. Even though Officer Trinket attempted to get everyone to calm down. Holly ignored them.

Splat. Millicent threw one of her cakes at Holly. "Why don't you go back to wherever you came from. You're not wanted!"

"Enough!" Charlene roared.

But Holly couldn't be stopped. She ran toward Millicent, whose face widened in horror at what she knew was coming, but she couldn't react fast enough.

Holly lifted the cheesecake in the air.

17

HOLLY SMASHED THE chocolate chip cheesecake in Millicent's face. "That's for breaking into my apartment today!"

Millicent spluttered, wiping the cake from her face.

Holly whirled around at Officer Trinket. "If that's not indicative of motive, I don't know what is. Maybe Millicent should spend a night in jail."

Trinket's gaze darted past Holly. That was the first clue. Before she ducked out of the way, Millicent brought a Jell-O salad down on top of Holly's head and rammed into her. They crashed to the floor.

They rolled one way and then the other. Cheesecake and Jell-O went in their hair and on their clothes as they wrestled.

Charlene pulled Holly off Millicent. "Enough, you two. No one messes with my famous Jell-O salad."

"That's right," Kitty said. "There was that one time—" Charlene shushed her friend with a look. "Maybe that's a story for another time."

Millicent and Holly stood, panting, staring at each other. The hurt from Millicent's betrayal that first day bubbled up. "Why would you be so mean? What did I ever do to you?"

"I'm sorry. Okay?" Millicent wiped at her eyes, the tears falling. "I broke into your cheesecake shop the other morning to taste the competition. My dad has worked hard to build up his business. But when I saw the body in the kitchen, I figured—"

"That you'd frame me for murder?"

"No! I promise. The only thing I'm guilty of is using a little hyperbole."

"A little?" Holly muttered. She pointed at the scrape hidden by cheesecake. "What about earlier today? And don't tell me it's research for your novel."

Millicent lowered her head in appropriate humility. "Every chef has a journal with their recipes. I was just looking around." Her head shot back up. "I'm sorry for that, but make no mistake. We're not going to be friends, Holly Hart."

Madeleine came up alongside her. "Come on, let's go, Millie."

"Hold on one second," Officer Trinket interrupted. "You were at the crime scene? Did you notice anything?"

"W-well..." Millicent stuttered.

"We can take this downtown."

"I'm sorry! I stepped closer to see the body, who it was, and I accidentally smudged a footprint in the frosting." She dropped her voice to a whisper. "It was a man's. But Papa wears loafers. This was a dress shoe."

Holly immediately thought of Mason Carlton.

***

A WET NOSE and stinky breath nudged Holly awake the next morning. She groaned and rolled the other way.

148

Persistent, Muffins jumped over her, frolicking like a newborn pup.

"Okay, okay. I get the message." Holly sat and pulled Muffins into her lap. "At least you didn't run away this morning." What did her little dog witness the morning of Ralph's murder? If only dogs spoke human. "That's one mystery that will never be solved."

Muffins whimpered.

"I know. You're hungry." Holly stretched, then, moving slowly, slipped a sweatshirt over her froggy pajamas and shuffled toward the kitchen. She giggled, thinking of the night before. What a mess! Charlene was sure to uninvite her to the mystery book club. In fact, she expected her to show up any minute.

In the kitchen, she poured Muffins his dog food and filled his water bowl, then she got started on breakfast. She made extra coffee, and using cheesecake filler in the freezer, threw together strawberry cheesecake muffins and popped them in the oven.

Coffee made, and a warm mug in her hand, Holly sat at the table with paper and pencil. It always helped her to make lists and then draw connections.

First, she jotted down Ralph's name, and her name. It grieved her to do so but she was smack dab in the middle of this. Off to the side, she wrote down the Carltons, Mason in particular. Madeleine seemed a little too nice in a superficial kind of way to pull off murder. Unless it was an act. She tapped her pencil on the table. That was something to think about.

As far as Mason was concerned, motive was lacking. She added a question mark next to his name. Why would he off two employees? On the other side of Ralph's name she wrote Millicent. She was connected to both herself and Ralph. A much stronger connection. And she was tight with Madeleine. And she just happened to pop up at both crime scenes. She drew another line connecting Millicent and Mason.

Too many unanswered questions. Some piece of this was missing, something that would reveal the right connections and lead to the murderer. The buzzer on the oven dinged as someone knocked on the door.

"Come on in!" Holly called, slipping her hand into an oven mitt. She opened the oven door, the delicious smell wafting out. "You're a little late."

"What are you—clairvoyant?" Charlene grumbled, walking inside with her shuffling gait.

"Nope. Not a bit." Holly placed a plate of muffins on the table, poured Charlene a mug, and refreshed her own. "Wish I was, then I would've known that you and Officer Trinket were related. I would've known to stay home last night. I would know a lot of things."

"But you expected me this morning?" Charlene sat and picked up the mug in her weathered hands, breathing in the nutty aroma.

"After last night? Yes. Figured we'd need to do some brainstorming over this mystery." She pushed her paper toward Charlene. "I already got started."

Charlene didn't even look at it. "We'll get to that in a minute. Let's talk about last night, first."

Holly sighed. "I'm sorry. I ruined your guest speaker's presentation. I brought in all sorts of drama. I messed up your house and floor. Never mind the Jell-O salad. I made a bad impression on all your friends." She took in a breath. "I completely understand if you'd rather I not come to any more book clubs." To grieve losing a circle of friends she'd just met, Holly bit into a muffin. "Hmm. My best yet."

Charlene stayed silent. With slow and careful actions, she chose a muffin and ate it, taking small bites. "I can see why Millicent is worried."

"I don't. Her father runs a complete bakery. Cheesecake is just one item he offers. He brings in the daily customers. I'm focusing on cheesecake, hence the name. My business and specialty desserts will appeal to the upper crust of the town. Cheesecake is perfect for high-class events. The kind where people are willing to drop thirty bucks on a delectable treat. I'll only be open several days a week, but I'll always be on call for custom orders."

"I guess we'll see over time."

Holly bit back her worries. She sounded a lot more confident than she felt about *Just Cheesecake*. "So, about last night."

Charlene sipped her coffee and finished her muffin, still not commenting on Holly's rash and rude behavior the previous night.

"You're driving me crazy. Go ahead and rant and rave. I know you're dying to." Holly braced herself for the worst.

"I talked with the girls, and we agreed." Charlene added in a long pause, which at this point, Holly suspected was for effect. "Last night was the most fun we'd had in a while, watching you two whippersnappers fight it out."

"What?" That was the last thing Holly expected Charlene to say. "But the mess?"

"Who cares? We got it cleaned up. And it was fun watching two girls fight over the attention of my son. Warms a mother's heart."

Holly tried to get the words out but stared in shock. They'd been fighting about a lot more than Charlene's son, but then again, Charlene often brought things around to Trent.

"That's right. You heard me correctly. Trent's a hunk. You two single, attractive women realize that on some level. Millicent's been after my son for months and now she's got some competition. This isn't just about cheesecake."

Holly knew better than to deny it. That would only fuel the fire of Charlene's imagination. Yes, Officer Trinket was definitely good looking, but he was a cop. Holly did not date cops. She refused to consider it. "I'm grateful you're being so gracious about last night. I promise it won't happen again."

"Don't make promises you can't keep." She tapped Holly's visual map. "Now, about this."

Holly started in, recapping the main suspects, herself included, their connections to each other, the victims, and the crime scene. "Something isn't adding up."

"I agree, and I know what we're missing."

Holly leaned forward, curious. "You knew this whole time and you didn't tell me right away?"

"I was feeling you out. Wanted to make sure you were the trustworthy sort." Charlene lowered her voice. "Our book club is more than your typical book club. We're an entire network of information. We're the unofficial, secret department of the Fairview police force."

Holly suppressed a chuckle because Charlene meant every word. "What does Officer Trinket think?"

"He couldn't fight crime without us, and he knows it." Charlene huffed, almost as if recounting all the arguments she'd had with her son over this secret crime-fighting force.

"Fine." Holly topped their mugs. "Explain to me how it works and how I earned your trust."

"You're passionate and you care. Kitty pointed out that you were an amateur sleuth in the making, and we should take you under our wing."

Holly laughed. "In other words you want to make sure I don't mess up your own sleuthing."

"That's right." Charlene offered a smile. "Like I said, we're a network of information. Kitty has a sister who works in the town office. Ann found a job last year with the janitorial company who cleans the police station and other important facilities." She wiggled her fingers. "A wealth of information right at our fingertips."

"Wow. And what role do you play?" Holly guessed Charlene was the commander, the leader, the boss. Someone who lit the fire of everyone's motivation.

"Thought that was obvious. Trent can't resist my Sunday pot roasts."

"In which you grill him for information?" Holly smiled, imagining how that must drive him nuts.

Charlene sniffed. "I wouldn't say grill. I'd say it's more of a subtle interrogation."

Right. Holly debated that. "Sounds like your secret society is complete. Why do you need me?"

"Oh, we could use a caterer, or possibly, a young attractive woman to infiltrate certain scenes."

"You mean like the Carlton's dinner party tonight?" Holly asked.

"You're smart too." Charlene reached back and pulled a pile of glittery material from her bag. "Put this on. It used to be Ann's. We don't have much time. Mason is having brunch. With some of your youthful flirting and charm, you need to finagle an invitation out of him."

Holly faked a yawn. "Already done."

"What?"

Holly loved that she caught Charlene by surprise. "I mean I already have an invitation to the party."

"Are you cheating on my son with this fellow?" Charlene accused.

"Officer Trinket and I are not dating. Nor shall we."

Charlene waved her off. "You're in denial. I see how it is." She pushed the dress toward Holly. She winked. "Wear this. It's perfect. And," Charlene whispered, "Kitty found that missing piece to this mystery. You should know before going undercover tonight."

Holly leaned forward, listening, curious.

"Ralph and Joseph were both recently hired by the Carltons. Their house is part of a group of homes that someone has been slowly buying up. The Carltons are finishing the paperwork for a new business endeavor. It's your job tonight to find information that reveals how it all connects."

WHAT HAD STARTED as a simple dinner party invitation from one of her first friends in Fairview had turned into a full undercover operation. Holly spent the rest of the day cleaning, reading, staying busy—anything to distract her from the coming night.

Before talking with Charlene, Holly had felt nervous about the party. She knew Mason from that upper crust society. That was it. She'd be a stranger, the newcomer. That society was about price tags and gossip and snobbery. It was about the size of yachts and the number of houses and trips around the world. But worse, it was about fakery and betrayal. She had no desire to immerse herself in it again.

Now? She had to find time to slip away and investigate.

If she were to be honest with herself, she'd planned on snooping around anyway, but now it was more official, and she felt the pressure. The whole investigation hinged on her success tonight.

Holly held the glittering sapphire dress in front of her body while looking in the mirror. Even though she'd laughed off Charlene's offer to wear Ann's dress, it was absolutely gorgeous. Her size too.

After spritzing a flowery body spray on her neck, Holly slipped into the dress. It fit in all the right places, hugging her body. Slowly, in a lame attempt to stall leaving for the party, Holly took her time with her makeup and hair. She pulled most of it up in a clip, leaving strands to curl down around the back of her neck.

"You can do this," she stated to herself in the mirror.

Before finding an excuse not to go at all, Holly gathered her supplies into her purse. Her phone had Charlene's, Kitty's, and Ann's numbers on speed dial. She had specific instructions to take pictures of any suspicious-looking documents and send them to Charlene right away.

Someone knocked on the door just as Holly gripped the knob. "Don't worry, Charlene..." She let her words trail off at the sight of Officer Trinket standing in her doorway.

He was out of uniform, dressed in dark jeans and a blue shirt. Holly's heart flip-flopped. Quickly, she shook it off. Charlene was planting ideas in her head. That was all.

"What has my mom dragged you into?" he asked, his gaze taking her in. "And wow, do you look terrific."

Holly stumbled back, aware at how close she'd been standing to him. She stuttered out her answer. "Um, thanks."

He stepped into the room, which all of a sudden seemed much too small. "Seriously. This has my mom written all over it." He narrowed his eyes, like he was putting it all together. "She invited you into that secret society of hers, didn't she?"

"Secret society?" Holly laughed but it sounded a little too fake to convince anyone. She drifted over to the fridge, turning her back to him. "Would you like something to drink? Water?"

She felt his warm grip on her bare arm. He flipped her around, so she almost crashed into his chest. For a moment, she lost her breath. He seemed to need a moment too.

"I'm serious. Did she put you up to something? Don't you listen to a word she says." He pursed his lips, then said, "If you go tonight, then I'll be your date. That's the only way you're going to that party. Someone needs to keep an eye on you."

She waved him off, but on the inside, seethed that he threw out commands like she was a genie in a bottle. It would be a disaster anyway. "Secret society? Last I checked we didn't live inside a thriller novel. Your mom can't stand me after the disaster I caused last night." Time was running short. She had to leave. Before he'd arrived, she already had stalled. "But while you're here, would you mind checking a leak in my bathroom sink? I'm afraid I'm going to wake up tomorrow morning with a flood in my house."

"Yes, I'll look at it, but we're not done talking about this. These investigations are dangerous. Especially at this stage of the game." He walked down the hall and into the bathroom. "No one should be meddling with a murder investigation, except for the police."

Quickly, regretting that he'd be furious at her, she followed with a kitchen chair in-hand. With Trent's head stuck under the sink, Holly closed the door and stuck the chair under the knob.

"Sorry!" she yelled, running for the door. "Take care of him, Muffins."

He barked his goodbyes as Trent banged on the bathroom door, calling out Holly's name.

***

HOLLY STOOD OUTSIDE, staring up at the Carlton house. Lights shone in all the windows. Party goers, Mason's friends and family, passed by, giving Holly snapshots of the party. With a tinge of sadness she thought of her family and friends, the ones she'd left behind when she ran away. Her nice, simple life she thought she'd been running toward had turned out to be anything but that.

She texted Charlene. *Going in.*

With a deep breath, she strode up to the front before she lost her nerve. For some crazy reason, she believed Millicent's claim of innocence with the murders. She believed her about the smudged footprint in the frosting. A dress shoe. That didn't automatically make the Carltons guilty, but that information along with Kitty's tip on a secret business deal, made this family worth looking into. The cops could only get so far.

Sometimes it took an amateur. Someone not held to the strict rules of investigative procedure. Someone who could slip in and out the rooms, like a shadow, unnoticed, invisible. Someone who had an in with the family, already invited to their dinner party.

Before she could knock on the door, it opened. Walter Huffly, with his kind eyes and portly figure, stepped back. "Greetings." He paused, a hand running through his beard. "Forgive me, I forget the name."

"Holly." She smiled graciously.

"Ah, yes, Ms. Holly. Forgive my forgetfulness. I assume you would be looking for Mason?" He ushered her inside, and the door closed behind her, a dull thud of finality. "I believe you'll find him in the great room, down the hall and to the left. He clicked his heels and nodded his head. "Nice to see you again."

The hallway stretched before her, wide and spacious, the walls lined with oil portraits of past generations, current family, and a beautiful rendition of the house. A large bouquet of flowers sat on a table. A plush oriental runner felt cushy under her uncomfortable, pointy heels. As she stood at the brink of the great room, Holly wished she'd worn flats.

At first, she stayed on the fringes of the party. Circling the room, looking for Mason, but definitely distracted by memories of the past. She took it in, the glitter and glam of the party, the social chatter—meaningless and boring, the sparkle of jewelry, the bored men drinking to pass the time, and the high giggles of younger women.

Finally, a warm hand touched her back. "I was wondering when you'd show up. Did you get lost?"

Holly turned to see Mason's friendly smile and the gleam of friendship in his eyes. Possibly more? "I got lost in the forest of opulence between the front door and the great room, but after battling a family of trolls and slaying a dragon, I finally made it."

He laughed. "Not only gorgeous but witty. Come. Have a drink." He grabbed a glass of white wine from a tray and placed it in her hand.

"Thank you." Fighting off the blush at his compliment, she walked through the partygoers with him. They parted like the Red Sea, like Mason was Moses. They said hello and offered him smiles. "I can see they look up to you. Do any of them really know you?"

He sipped his cocktail. "Ah, such an insightful question. Is the rest of the night going to be this tough?"

"Nah. I'll take it easy on you." But still, she waited, hoping he'd answer.

After introducing her to several couples their age, forcing her into the shallow conversation of a party like this, she asked again. "How many do you consider your close friends?"

He took another sip as if to stall. "To be honest. I let very few in." He quickly tried to explain. "Not that I can't let them in, but after years of having friends really only drawn to me because of my family's name, I have become rather cynical." He leaned closer to her. "Which is why the start of my friendship with you was such a fresh breeze. You knew nothing. Not my name. Nor my wealth."

Unfortunately, Holly didn't have a good answer for him. "It must be tough."

Again, she was grateful for her friendship with Charlene, and even Officer Trinket, or Trent. After locking him in her bathroom, they could probably move to a first name basis. That reminded her of her mission.

She cleared her throat. "You mentioned working from home. Do you find it tough to stay focused?"

"At first, I did, but over time, I learned to block out the distractions. Now I love it. I find myself more distracted when I commute to the office."

"Then, surely, you must have a private office." She laughed. "And you must not have any pets." If she had to work from home, Muffins would never let her get any work done.

"No pets. But yes, I took over my father's office."

"Hopefully near the kitchen?" He looked puzzled, so she added, "Easy access to snacks."

"Oh, right. Definitely. My office is almost right across the hall."

Bingo. Now she just had to find the kitchen and then locate his office. First, she had to escape Mason. She'd figured that would be easy enough, after all, he was the host. But no. Wherever he went, whomever he chatted with, he tugged Holly along, introducing her and plying her with wine.

Turning down a third glass, she hiccupped. "Excuse me. I must use the little girl's room."

He nodded and continued his conversation. She slipped away, across the room, and exited into a different hallway where the waiters were exiting and entering. She followed one until he turned right into the kitchen. And then, swallowing her guilt about breaking Mason's trust, she continued down the hall.

The first few doors she tried opened into various sitting and sunrooms. Nothing that looked like an office or a study. Finally, the last door she tried she found success.

Bookshelves lined the room, filled with leather-bound volumes and collections. A stately oak desk sat by the window, uncluttered and clean.

Adrenaline surged at the thought of solving the mystery, of finding justice for Ralph, and for Joseph. Everyone deserved justice.

She crept into the room and shut the door behind her.

NOT WANTING TO turn on the lights, she pressed the flashlight on her phone. The small beam cut through the darkness, revealing Mason's desk. She headed right toward it, light on her feet, breath shallow with nerves.

She ran a hand over the smooth, polished surface. "Okay, Mason. Where are your secrets?" she whispered. "Sorry to do this."

The top of the desk held nothing but a few framed photos, an oval paperweight, and a desk calendar. So much for finding evidence right away, she scolded herself. Of course it wouldn't be that easy. Especially during a party. The papers would be tucked away in a drawer, probably locked. She tried the first one.

Locked!

Not one to give up, Holly slid open the shallow drawer that held compartments for pens, pencils, and rulers. As her light flashed over, she saw a glimpse of silver. The key.

With a glance at the door, and pausing to listen for footsteps, she snatched the key and unlocked the top drawer. It slid open effortlessly. Her heart thumping, Holly rifled through the stack of file folders. She grabbed the top one and opened it on the desk. Tax receipts. She took a few pictures, but nothing appeared suspicious.

She attacked the second folder and then the third. Nothing. The last one seemed a bit heavier, thicker. She opened it, wiping her sweaty palms on her dress. The light shining on it, the first paper was a blueprint of some sort. So weren't the next few. She spread them out on the desk, piecing them together like a puzzle. It appeared to be a huge building of sorts. Quickly, she snapped a photo.

At the top, in small, capitalized print was a title. One that brought understanding and disappointment. She zoomed in and snapped another picture.

Deep inside, Holly had hoped that she wouldn't find anything. That Mason and his family would be innocent. That evidence would come to light that steered suspicion onto someone else.

Under the blueprints, were typed sheets, page after page. One glance told her it was a business plan with estimated financials, timelines, and property to be acquired. She snapped another photo.

The door clicked. Someone was entering.

She doused the light and ducked behind the desk. No time to put away the blueprints and files. Her guilty actions available for anyone to find. Breathing in and out, slowly, so she wouldn't give herself away, Holly realized she should have sent off the photos right away. Now, she didn't dare use her phone, the backlighting would give her away immediately.

Soft footsteps padded across the Oriental rug.

She thought about Trent, in her bathroom, locked up. Maybe she should've taken him up on his offer to accompany her. At the time, she saw it as another person to dodge. By now, he should've called someone to let him out.

"Someone's in here." The voice was masculine and soft, almost as if the person was trying to disguise it. "It's not very nice to snoop around in someone's house. In their private affairs."

Holly struggled to place the voice. She debated whether to pop up and claim she lost an earring after exploring a bit of the house. She debated whether to act drunk and claim to be lost. Instead, she froze. Unable to make the decision.

As he paced closer, the man continued. "I warned Mason off opening himself up to new friendships at this time. Too much at stake. Foolishly, he let a pretty face draw him in. Play him for the fool."

Holly stifled a gasp. Walter Huffly! No. Not the friendly man who always showed kindness, who played Santa Claus and donated to charities. Did Mason know what his father was into? That they were buying up properties for their grand idea of a Fairview Country Club? That his family used murder when one family didn't want to sell?

The light flicked on, a bright, unwavering spotlight shining directly on her. Or that's what it felt like.

Walter stepped closer.

Not ready to give up, Holly gripped the cold metal of the desk chair. If she could only slip out and have enough time to text Charlene, everything would be okay. They would come for her.

As Walter stepped around the desk, Holly noticed his black dress shoes, recently shined. She shoved the chair as hard as she could right at him. With a grunt, he was caught off balance and stumbled back.

Now was her chance. Scrambling to her feet, she rushed around the desk and smacked into a hard wall. Except it wasn't a wall. It was Mason.

This time the words came easily. "Gosh, I lost my way trying to find the bathroom and then dropped my earring. Thought it rolled under the desk here but I couldn't find it anywhere."

Any gleam of kindness or friendship had disappeared from Mason's eyes. They were cold and flat, and pierced through Holly's lies. At the same time, she detected a hint of sadness and betrayal.

She had one option. "I'm sorry, Mason."

Walter huffed behind her. "Don't let her sweet talk you again!"

"What are you sorry for?" Mason asked.

Holly tried to stall, keep him talking. Maybe she could inch to the side and then make a dash for the door. "Sorry that this friendship almost worked out. Sorry that whether you knew it or not, your family was playing dirty. Sorry you

171

weren't the man I hoped you were. One of honesty and integrity."

Unfortunately, Mason denied nothing. She saw in the way he held his body straight and rigid, that long ago he'd accepted his family for what they were. He might've been shocked at first, but then slowly, over time, had to accept it.

"There is another way," Holly whispered. "Confess and cooperate."

"Sorry, Holly."

Danger reflected in his eyes. Walter brought his arm back, a paperweight clutched in his hand. He swung. She ducked. He hit nothing but air. The force whirled him around until he banged into the wall.

Glad for her pointy heels, she kicked Mason's shin then dashed past him. Freedom flickered briefly until his hand clamped down on her arm. He yanked her back into the room.

Walter took charge. "Mason, you know what to do."

Obediently, like a puppy, he took all the papers from the folder and passed them through the shredder.

"Mason, you don't have to do this." Holly attempted to win him over. He'd been drawn into a way of life, a way of greed and power.

"Shut up," Walter snarled. He pulled a pistol from the back of his pants. He clicked off the safety and pointed it at Holly. "Too bad you couldn't mind your own business."

Swallowing down her nerves, Holly blew on her fingernails in an attempt to show that she didn't care. "Too bad shredding those papers won't do you a bit of good."

Walter hesitated. His eyes darkened as he sized up Holly.

"Too bad I took photos and already sent them to Officer Trinket." She glanced past Walter as if Trent should be bursting into the room any second. "He should be on his way now. In fact, he probably already has the place surrounded."

"You're bluffing." Walter chuckled. It sounded fake and forced.

Holly detected the shortness of breath. He was nervous. If he was nervous then he might not take the time to think through his responses. She held up her phone. "You can see it right here. Just come and look."

He narrowed his eyes. "I'm not stupid. Toss me the phone."

The shredding machine whirred as Mason continued to destroy the evidence. "What? I can't hear you!" Holly shouted.

"Throw me the phone."

"Okay." She slid it gently, so it stopped halfway between them.

Walter growled, but stepped forward to snatch it off the floor. As soon as he bent over, Holly kicked, heel first, so the sharp point landed in Walter's neck.

A hiss of pain escaped his mouth. He stumbled back and clamped his hand against his skin, torn and bleeding where she'd kicked him. He pulled his hand away. His eyes widened. His face paled at the sight of blood. He looked like he was about to be sick. But as he wiped the blood off on his pants, he focused on her. A vein throbbed at his temple. His hands trembled even as he curled them into fists.

"That's it," he roared and rushed Holly. His body rammed into hers.

She flailed her arms and tried to fight back, but he was like a locomotive. She slammed into the bookshelf with his full weight following. The air knocked from Holly's chest. She doubled over, gasping. Sharp pain pierced her lungs with each breath. Finally, after a deep breath she straightened, wobbling on her feet. Ready for a second attack.

Walter towered over her. Sweat beaded on his forehead. His eyes bulged, the crazy swirling in their depths. He lifted

174

his arm back. Oh God, he was going to slug her. She made fists ready to punch him in the gut with everything she had left. A sudden motion at the door caught her eye.

"Look!" Holly pointed behind Walter's back.

Trent rushed into the room, Charlene, Kitty, and Ann right behind him. Trent tackled Walter. They fell to the ground, a flurry of arms and legs. Walter struggled. He fought back. He grunted out threats.

Running off adrenaline and experience, Trent overpowered him. He whipped out the cuffs and read him his rights. Mason tried to escape, but Charlene and the girls stood at the door, an impenetrable wall.

After slapping cuffs on Walter, Trent was at her side. "I should arrest you, too."

She wanted to muster up a wise crack, but somehow, the words deserted her. "Thank you." Her voice cracked, the reality of what happened hitting her.

He pulled her into his arms. "But I'm just too darn thankful right now that you're okay."

Charlene winked at her.

Holly mumbled into Trent's shirt. "I'm glad you're not one of the bad guys."

"What?" He eased her away. Immediately, she missed the feeling of warmth and safety.

"So you're not working with them?"

"No," he whispered, hugging her again. "I'm one of the good guys. Promise."

HOLLY AND CHARLENE stood outside *Just Cheesecake.* The day had started with brilliant sunshine and a few fluffy clouds. Warmth tinged the air, and excitement surged up through Holly. She giggled.

"What do you have to be so giddy about?" Charlene asked. "We have a busy day ahead of us, especially since you wrangled me into helping you."

Holly huffed. "Wrangled?"

"That's right. You caught me in a moment of weakness and conned me into it. You've been working me like a horse these past few days."

Holly smiled and thought back on last week at the Carlton house when everything exploded. It had taken a couple days to recover from the shock of near death, of facing Mason, someone she thought was a potential friend. Walter Huffly, the mastermind behind the Carlton business venture to build a Fairview country club, had held a gun to her. Driven by greed, he'd wanted success so badly he'd resorted to murder in order to buy the last house. A project he'd worked years on, investing thousands of hours. Then, he smashed open her lock and dumped the body, effectively framing her for murder. Or at least, making her a potential suspect, a distraction, a red herring. It had nothing to do with her. He hadn't even known her. The use of her cheesecake mashed in the man's face was just for effect.

Murder was a terrible business.

"I can see it on your face. Read you like my favorite mystery novel. Stop rehashing the whole nasty affair," Charlene reprimanded.

"I know. You're right. But today, the Grand Opening, the one postponed when this whole mess started, brings back memories." After unlocking the door, she stopped. "It also reminds me how thankful I am for friends. Like you."

"Oh, stop with the mushy stuff. I don't want my makeup to smudge."

Holly laughed. "You don't wear makeup."

"That, my dear, is entirely beside the point."

They entered *Just Cheesecake* and dove into preparations. Charlene rolled out the cart that held the free samples. Something to draw customers inside. The plan being that even if they didn't make a purchase today, they'd remember the exquisite taste of her mini cheesecakes and sample cheesecake brownies, and return another day.

Holly studied the room. Everything gleamed and shined with their hard work. The glass showcase held all her tasty goodies, several kinds of cheesecakes and muffins. She even had everything marked down twenty percent. More encouragement for newcomers to feel the pressure to purchase.

"Stop your worrying." Charlene stood next to her. "You've done everything you can. Enjoy it today."

"Easy for you to say." Holly ignored the nervous flutters in her stomach. "We open in thirty minutes." She also wondered what Millicent might do to sabotage her opening day. She'd put nothing past her.

Holly headed back to the kitchen to check one last time. When she returned to the storefront, Kitty and Ann had arrived, coffees in-hand.

Kitty smiled. "The place looks great. We thought we'd toast with an appropriate breakfast beverage. To not only the start of a successful business, but for being the one to capture the evidence on her phone that solved the mystery. For risking life and limb to bring justice."

"Okay, okay, we get the point." Charlene helped pass out the coffees. "We're opening soon."

"To a successful venture and opening day," Kitty stated.

"To delicious desserts," Ann said.

"To solving murders." Charlene held her coffee in the air.

Holly lifted hers too. "To friends."

The group broke up, Kitty and Ann making the first official purchases of the day. Holly offered them freebies, but they refused. Charlene put on her apron, grumbling.

With a smile, Holly wiped down the front counter one last time and checked the cash register. The photos from her phone had been given to the police. They revealed the business plans of the Carltons and enough evidence for a conviction. That's what Trent said. But what was even better than solving a murder... She had friends. Real ones.

Someone knocked on the door. Already? She looked up to see Trent's smile. Ignoring Charlene's smirk, Holly unlocked the door and stepped outside. "Hello, there."

Trent shifted awkwardly on his feet, his hands behind his back. "I wanted to wish you good luck today. And I wanted to give you this." He revealed a long-stemmed rose in a slender vase. "Something to brighten your kitchen or your home."

"Thank you," she whispered, accepting the gift. She couldn't believe she'd thought Trent could be a dirty cop, working for the Carltons by overlooking their affairs.

"I would've stopped in earlier, but you've been busy readying for the big day."

"And you've been up to your ears in paperwork for closing the case."

"True." He ran a hand through his hair, making it stick out on the sides.

"Um." Holly pointed to his hair and laughed. "You have a piece..."

"What?" He messed up the rest of his hair and then flashed her an innocent look. "Is something out of place?"

Hesitantly, she smoothed his hair. "Better. Kind of."

Trent straightened. "I wanted to officially wish you good luck on your opening day. And...make sure the kitchen was clear of bodies."

"Thank you. Everything was just how we left it last night. And Muffins has managed to not run away all week. This evening I'll take him on a long walk. Maybe to the park."

"Good. Then the next thing on my list is to make a purchase at a new shop in town. Have you heard of it?"

Holly liked this flirty Officer Trinket. "Oh, I might have." She peered to the right and to the left, pretending to look for it. When she lifted her head straight up to the Grand Opening banner, she laughed. "I found it! Why don't you come on in? We're about to open!"

"Good," he muttered. "You can focus on your business instead of solving crime."

With her back to him, acting like she didn't hear, Holly smiled a secret smile. She wasn't making any promises. Every crime, murder or not, demanded justice. That passion burned in Holly along with the desire to bake, and to own a successful business.

She flipped the sign to Open, then called, "*Just Cheesecake* is officially open for business!"

THE END

THE END

About the Author

Laura Pauling writes about spies, murder, and mystery. She is the author of the Baron & Graystone Mysteries and the Holly Hart Cozy Mystery Series. She loves the puzzle of a whodunnit and witty banter between characters. In her free time, she likes to read, walk, bike, snowshoe, and spend time with family or enjoy coffee with friends. She writes to entertain, experience a great story, explore issues of friendship and forgiveness and...work in her jammies and slippers.

Visit Laura at http://laurapauling.com to sign up for her newsletter or send her a message through the contact tab. Or email her directly at laura@laurapauling.com.

Made in United States
Troutdale, OR
10/05/2024

23438962R00110